Published in Great Britain by

L.R. Price Publications Ltd, 2024

27 Old Gloucester Street,

London, WC1N 3AX

www.lrpricepublications.com

Cover artwork by L.R. Price Publications Ltd

Copyright © 2024

Used under exclusive and unlimited licence by

L.R. Price Publications Ltd.

ISBN: 978-1-915330-98-7

The Most Sought After Woman in Rome

Philip E. Rowson

L.R. Price Publications Ltd

The Meeting

"Why should I repent when the most powerful men in Rome are knocking on my door?" The speaker was Fillide Melandroni, a young courtesan of Rome in the late 16th century. "Cardinals, bankers, artists, centurions of the legion - they don't want me to change. They don't say to me, 'Stop what you're doing, it's sinful.' They say, 'I'm coming to see you again.' This is what happens."

It takes some nerve to explain yourself like this to a senior priest from the Vatican when you're only eighteen and living in a city which is calm and orderly one day, in violent uproar the next. But this was Fillide, and more often than not, she knew what was going to happen next.

The Vatican declared her Cortigiana Scandalosa (scandalous courtesan) for refusing to repent and take the Sacrament. Courtesans were liable to be seized in the street and dealt some very rough justice, but Fillide was confident she'd survive.

She took pride in her ability to manipulate situations to her advantage; so successful was she in this, that she was there at the start, building an institution that's alive and kicking in Italian and American society to this day. There are many names for that institution: Cosa Nostra, the Mob, and, most notably, the Mafia.

All of that and more would come to pass. First, she had a part to play in the lives of two of the greatest artists of the day: Caravaggio and Peter Paul Rubens, as well as two Popes, three Cardinals, one Knight of Malta, the architect of St Peter's Square and the infamous Cesare Borgia, Captain-General of the Papal Army.

Caravaggio was delighted with her intrusion, Rubens in despair. Pope Paul V was sympathetic, Pope Julius II and Cardinal Baronius eternally grateful, Cardinals Colonna and del Monte less so. Cesare Borgia cursed her with his dying breath.

We begin at an early stage in her career before Caravaggio and Rubens had met, though they were about to.

"Come this way Giovanotto, there's someone I want you to meet," Cardinal del Monte said to Rubens. The young artist with a growing reputation had heard about Caravaggio, the man he was sure the Cardinal was talking about. In the gossiping art world of Rome, Caravaggio was the latest sensation. But not all the talk was about his work. Stories of wild behaviour and bad-tempered outbursts were a significant part of the growing legend. Caravaggio was alleged to patrol the streets at night dressed in black. He kept to the shadows to avoid unwanted attention but often achieved the opposite by starting a loud argument, which would sometimes develop into a physical attack. In every way possible, he was contrary.

This was happening while Caravaggio was staying as a privileged guest in the del Monte household. The Cardinal was an ambassador for the powerful Florentine Medici family. They paid for the upkeep of his apartments, and he advised them on art decoration for their palaces. He was one of Rome's leading patrons: a key figure, and someone every artist was keen to cultivate. As usual, Rubens had an inside track. He was staying with his brother who worked as a librarian for Cardinal Colonna, a senior member of a powerful Roman family who had given him a letter of introduction to del Monte.

Rubens had heard the story of how Caravaggio attracted attention when he first arrived in Rome as a struggling artist. He painted street scenes that del Monte might recognise and displayed them close to his home. The paintings showed scenes of temptation: prosperous young men, for example, about to be duped by cheating chancers. But these were no ordinary works; they displayed Caravaggio's talent for capturing those moments of danger and drama, warning viewers about what might happen. Del Monte judged that

Caravaggio's insight would be even more impressive if it were applied to biblical scenes in church decoration. He was right, and this was one of the foundations of Caravaggio's commercial success; del Monte's influence won him many church commissions.

The Cardinal took him under his wing, even though he knew about Caravaggio's talent for getting into trouble; but maybe this appealed to del Monte. Church figures often led a double life, and there was a thriving underworld in Rome, close to the top reaches of society.

Although Rubens knew he was in dangerous company with Caravaggio, this was a man he could learn from. He admired the audacity of Victorious Cupid, Caravaggio's life-size, full-frontal portrait of a naked boy. The plump, mischievous figure is smiling and laughing, offering a basket of fruit to the viewer. Or is it sex that's on offer? Rubens would never paint a picture like that, he was too conservative, but he enjoyed the outrage it created. The Roman banker who commissioned it kept his Cupid hidden behind a curtain, bringing it out for special guests he trusted. Maybe the painting was innocent, but Rubens didn't think so. He could see that it offered a choice of narratives: some of the fruit was rotten and could have been a warning about the temptations of sex. Or, just as likely, it flaunted the joy of sex.

When the two artists were alone Caravaggio tried to tease information from him, thinking he might be a rival for the Cardinal's patronage. "We painters have a duty to present the realities of life in all its forms, don't we?" he asked. "Most of my work is for the Church. I bring fresh life to Bible stories so that people who can't read can suddenly understand them better. I always go for that moment of revelation. But there is life with many experiences and pleasures outside of the Church. Do you agree?" Rubens knew the wisest answer to that one. Caravaggio was questioning him in a direct, aggressive way but he wasn't going to be provoked. "Yes, it's our duty to teach many lessons in life, so long as we stay within the teachings of the holy script," he replied. "But life isn't simple and straightforward is it?"

"When I say all of it, I mean all of it!" Caravaggio shouted, standing up and laughing at the same time, showing he understood the diplomacy. The mischief-maker in him suddenly thought it would be amusing to shock this earnest Flemish artist, teach him different lessons. "Maybe we can take a stroll together one night and I'll show you all of Rome." That was how Rubens ended up sitting in a tavern with Caravaggio and Fillide Melandroni. Caravaggio had recently started using her as a model, but tonight she was agitated and drunk. She kept telling the men how she was going to attack a rival courtesan. "She's stolen one of my best customers, I'm going to teach her a lesson she'll remember." Caravaggio made no attempt to persuade her against it, saying to Rubens, "She's drunk, she doesn't mean it. When she's sober she's a very smart woman. They have a hard life here in Rome."

True enough, authorities often rounded up women off the streets, whipped and beat them, attempting to change their way of life. It seldom worked and many had pimps or influential clients to protect them. Fillide had both and one of them, her pimp Ranuccio Tomassoni, arrived to join them at the table. He wasn't pleased to see her condition. "Melandroni, you're a disgrace. Look at you, drunk again. Go home - you have work tomorrow, you cheap whore!"

"Not so cheap that I don't make you rich, brutto bastardo!" she cursed him angrily. This was a loss of face in front of Rubens that Tomassoni couldn't let go of. He moved around the table and tried to pull her to her feet, snarling "Get out, now!" Rubens instantly saw the other side of Caravaggio, who jumped to his feet and confronted Tomassoni. "She's with me and she stays," he shouted. "That's the way it is!" He emphasised the way he felt by pushing the pimp away from the table. "I have an important guest here from Flanders," he said, gesturing towards Rubens. "Don't act like a fool, you're the disgrace, not her. Go!"

Caravaggio was ready for violence and Tomassoni got the picture. He took in the prosperous-looking Rubens and decided it would go badly for him if he stayed. "I don't care for the company of drunken whores anyway, that's more your style," he shot back at Caravaggio, but made sure he was heading towards the door as he spoke. Turning to shout a curse at Fillide, he left hurriedly, vowing that one day he'd find a way to bring Caravaggio down. The rest of the evening was peaceful and Rubens enjoyed himself as other artists came to chat with them. There were questions for Caravaggio, mainly about his chiaroscuro technique, and mostly he answered with good humour - though not always. There were more flashes of temper and Rubens saw how quickly the atmosphere could change, usually when the conversation turned to gossip and got more personal. The danger was there for everyone to see, and the following day he found that Fillide had carried out her threat. She'd attacked her rival with a razor and was in court waiting to go before the judge. "This is the life and time of Caravaggio," Rubens said to his brother as he described the night to him. "The biggest mistake anyone could make is to let the problems of his life spill out into judgement of his art." "Caravaggio's art is his life. Raw, realistic, the art is the man. We can't have one without the other and no one I've seen in Flanders,

Paris or Rome has his vision and the skill to put it on canvas." It was a truthful judgement by Rubens - he spoke from the heart - but it was not one that authority could live with. Soon afterwards, Caravaggio was commissioned by Laerzio Cherubini, a Papal lawyer, to paint the death of Mary Magdalena for his chapel. The finished work, Death of the Virgin, was controversial and rejected by the client. His main problem with it was the frank treatment of Mary. With a drooping head, simple dress and swollen naked feet she looked too mortal, not idealised at all, not given enough respect. Most damning of all, though, was that Caravaggio was rumoured to have used a prostitute as his model. For Rubens, it was simply a masterful work by a man at the height of his powers. The scene was subdued, the picture portrayed silent grief: the shock that comes before tears. He used stillness, a feeling of silence to convey a different level of grief. A mixture of soft light and shadow added depth but most striking of all was the sudden, dazzling light that gave the virgin her supreme presence. Caravaggio captured the moment of realisation when grief is unendurable. "Art like this shouldn't be lost or forgotten", Rubens said as soon as he saw it. By recommending the work to his patron, Vincenzo Gonzaga, the Duke of Mantua, he made sure it wouldn't be. The Duke agreed with his judgement, bought it and instructed his ambassador to exhibit Death of the Virgin in Rome with strict instructions that it should never be copied. This was a masterpiece for him alone. Soon Caravaggio was beginning to influence the art of his age, introducing a new, energetic realism. His work was dramatised by the chiaroscuro effect introduced by Michelangelo, but Caravaggio developed the style further. Rubens felt the charge of his paintings and went on to use similar techniques throughout his career. Yet his life and style could not have been more different to the drama and violence that followed Caravaggio. Where Rubens was an artist with the charm of a diplomat, Caravaggio was the erratic disruptor of power; medieval police records show his long history of assault. Far from being put on trial, Rubens won the respect of many royal courts. He was chosen by Marie de Medicis, mother of King Louis XIII of France, to paint twenty-one pictures of episodes in her life. Yet despite their differences, Caravaggio enjoyed Rubens' company. Out of the blue, he visited Rubens with Fillide and a couple of artist friends and invited him to join them for a walk. "Andare a spasso, you'll enjoy it." This wasn't unusual. When he was in the mood he would set off with an entourage to tour the cafés. His friends were pleased to be invited. Occasionally some who had seen what could happen said "Thanks, but thanks."

More often they jumped at the chance to spend time with one of the celebrities of the age. Rubens joined in without hesitating. He'd come to Rome to learn, and this looked like an ideal occasion. As they went along, other artists joined them, as did the street people Caravaggio enjoyed. Some were criminal, others law-abiding, but none were the cream of Roman society. It was a bizarre mixture of intellectuals and street smarts, artists and artisans together with prostitutes looking for trade or simply out to enjoy themselves. Rubens recognised they were all there for whatever the night might bring. Laughter, arguments, or both. Definitely alcohol, probably sex. But, likeliest of all for Caravaggio, there was inspiration. Rubens watched as he gradually withdrew from conversation yet stayed in the middle of the crowd - and observed. This was how Caravaggio soaked up the scenes and characters for so many of his masterpieces. It was how he met most of his subjects: casually, on the streets. It was where he had first met Fillide Melandroni. He sensed that beneath the raw street chatter she used with clients there was an intelligence that looked far beyond her next encounter. When he suggested she model for him she asked, "Why?" "Because your face tells stories," he answered. "And it's full of contradictions. Beauty, yes, but other, more important things. If we work together, I might find them, and I want to try." She was intrigued, she'd never modelled for anyone before, and that was how their collaboration started. Some of his paintings were erotic and led to gossip, many had biblical themes and earned him good fees. One night, the inevitable happened and they went to bed together, more by chance than design. To her, he was exotic, removed from daily struggles and life on the edge. Their conversations strengthened her rebellious spirit and she thought more about the contrasting worlds she moved between. From the marble-floored palazzos of her rich clients to the colourful homes of prosperous traders, back to the earth and straw of the bars where labourers relaxed. Caravaggio described to her the joy he felt as he brought the grime and sweat of life to sacred biblical scenes. She sensed the anger that was never far from him, although she never felt threatened. She began to identify with the realism he sought but questioned why he risked his relationships by painting scenes he knew patrons wouldn't accept. She had a healthy respect for the fees he commanded as his fame spread. "Why did you have to put the horse's ass right at the front of the picture?" she demanded. "Why did you put it in at all?" "Because it expressed my opinion of the rest of the pictures in that church!" he told her and laughed. On this particular night, she decided to leave Caravaggio and Rubens when she saw her pimp, Tomassoni, was in the area. He had friends with him and she knew her presence would annoy him. Caravaggio and Tomassoni together meant trouble anyway and she didn't want to make it worse. Taking Rubens to one side, she said, "Can you do me a favour? Tomassoni is coming, so I'm leaving. Please try to keep Caravaggio calm." Rubens had a natural authority and she hoped his presence would inhibit Tomassoni. But, as the night went on, he joined the crowd and edged closer to Caravaggio. The atmosphere changed. Voices grew louder. Rubens, the future diplomat, always had a sense of duty, and as he watched the situation unfold, he felt he had to help. He hadn't been impressed by Tomassoni the first time he'd seen him, now he saw him as a foul-mouthed bully, bursting to start a fight. Tomassoni confronted Caravaggio in the street as they left a café. "So, I see you have your sword with you tonight; are you ready to use it or are you going to run away?" "Your mouth is doing all the running as usual," Caravaggio shot back. "As for running from you: never!" His hand was on his sword, anger and contempt for Tomassoni pushing him to the edge. Before the scene could develop any further, two of Caravaggio's friends stepped between the two men, facing Tomassoni. "Whatever the problem. It can wait till tomorrow," Mario Minitti, one of the painter's oldest friends said to Tomassoni. "We are meeting with friends, not looking for trouble." As a conversation started between Minitti and Tomassoni, Rubens pulled Caravaggio back from the crowd. "Come with me now," he urged. "This is a small man not worth a second of your time. Just leave him to his fantasies, it will be for the best." Unfortunately, Caravaggio was now beyond the reasoning stage, and Tomassoni was screaming that he wanted revenge, accusing the painter of insulting his wife. Caravaggio pushed Rubens away. "The time for diplomacy has gone. I have to settle things with this man tonight, he's insulting me, and he won't stop." Rubens tried again. "At least wait till tomorrow, my friend. We can deal with him then. Warn him it will go badly unless he stops this rubbish. He is nothing more than a common pimp and you are a commissioned artist with the most respected patrons in Rome. It's foolish to waste your time with him and risk so much. Come back to the house of del Monte with me and we'll have him thrown into prison for challenging you. He is nothing."

For Rubens, this was the obvious thing to do. He had no doubt that Cardinal del Monte could use his authority and Tomassoni would find himself in front of a judge, facing a prison sentence, or worse. "No, stay out of this. You are a stranger here, it's not for you to interfere," Caravaggio said, pushing Rubens away. "I don't want del Monte involved in this. There's no reason for him to hear anything about it." Rubens knew this wasn't true; Caravaggio was too well known. If he were involved in a street fight, all of Rome would soon hear about it. The shouting and pushing was getting violent and, reluctantly, Rubens decided there was nothing he could do. Caravaggio was acting true to form. He wouldn't listen to reason, but there were friends with him who lived locally and could better handle the situation. As for Rubens, if he got caught up in a street fight it could damage his relationships with his patrons. If the night went badly, though, he could be a witness and testify that Caravaggio was provoked beyond reason. The next morning, he discovered the worst. There had been a fight and Caravaggio had killed Tomassoni. Worse still, friends of Tomassoni got to the city magistrates first and told their story. According to them, "Caravaggio was out of control, he drew his sword and murdered an unarmed, innocent man for no reason." The artist was now on the run, wanted for murder. There were all kinds of theories about the bad blood between Caravaggio and Tomassoni. The erotic way he painted Fillide Melandroni started a rumour that he'd fallen for her and that they'd had sex. As her pimp, Tomassoni expected to be paid and Caravaggio refused. Another theory was that Caravaggio lusted after Tomassoni's wife Lavinia - and seduced her. Tomassoni may have discovered this alleged affair, or it could have been all about Melandroni. Either way, Tomassoni had a grievance and Caravaggio was not a man to back down. They both had a history of violence, so this was a fight waiting to happen.

The details of how Tomassoni died were confused. It could have been a fight between them or a mass brawl that went too far. Rubens couldn't be sure of the truth. The version he had heard was that Caravaggio got the better of the fight and knocked Tomassoni to the ground. According to Roman street culture of the day, if someone was involved with another man's woman, the loser of the fight was liable to have his penis cut off; it wasn't out of character for Caravaggio to do so. He held

Tomassoni down, and with a slash of his sword, castrated him. It would not necessarily be fatal but this was an enraged, possibly unhinged Caravaggio. He probably cut through an artery, leaving Tomassoni to bleed to death at the scene. "That sounds like it could be near the truth," Rubens said to his brother while discussing what they could do to help Caravaggio. "We'll never know if it was about money or sex, but, either way, I'm sure Caravaggio thought he could get away with it because of his status. Or maybe he just didn't care; that's the way he is. But I'm going to make sure Cardinal del Monte knows that Tomassoni started this. I was there, I saw it. I'm going to say that whatever happened after I left - Tomassoni started it, and this wasn't murder. There's no reason for Caravaggio to be on the run. He's done nothing wrong and I'm going to make sure everyone knows that."

Philip E. Rowson

Making of a revolutionary

Caravaggio lost his father and grandfather on the same day, to the bubonic plague that hit Milan when he was only six. Maybe this early loss of male mentors contributed to his lack of control in later life, but it didn't leave him without some benefits. His family had connections to the important Colonna dynasty, and they would shelter him later when there was a price on his head. The young boy's father had been an architect working for the Marchese of Caravaggio and, after his death, the family moved to Caravaggio, a small town near the city of Bergamo. His father's reputation and creative skills won him local apprenticeships and his own talents were soon recognised. But small-town life was never going to hold this erratic genius. He left for Rome when he was twenty-one, taking with him nothing more than the name he decided to adopt as his own. In characteristic style, Caravaggio's leaving was dramatic. He was fleeing from quarrels, including an 'incident' where he wounded a police officer. The future legend arrived in Rome, 'naked and needy, with nowhere to live and no money.'

To begin with, he had to work at hack jobs. He painted flowers and fruit in the studio of Guiseppe Cesari, the favourite artist of Pope Clement VIII. A lowly start, but already he was moving in the circles that counted. The fiery young artist was in the right place at the right time. New churches and palazzi were being built and needed decorations. One of the early pictures that attracted the attention of Cardinal del Monte was The Fortune Teller. It featured a gypsy girl and began Caravaggio's association with the ordinary street people of Rome. His choice of models led to some extraordinary art, but his thinking attracted criticism from conservative figures in the Church. For them, the images weren't aspirational, but Caravaggio's response was typically, "Why use classical models when nature has provided me with models like this?" It wasn't the answer critics were looking for. They wanted art to idealise religion, not drag it down to the streets. Fortunately for Caravaggio, other voices disagreed and commissioned work from him. But his outspoken comments about art and the Church made him many enemies who were happy to see him away from Rome.

The next news Rubens had of Caravaggio came from Paolo Francisco, an influential member of the Knights of Malta. The Knights were an ancient Catholic organisation who also had a military role. They usually worked alongside Catholic rulers, but recently they'd been involved in a power struggle against the Vatican. That's why, when Caravaggio was forced to flee from Rome, they'd taken him in. "We protected him when he was on the run," Francisco said. "He produced magnificent work for us, but then he had a nervous breakdown and broke our rules. We had to imprison him for his own sake, but his friends helped him to escape. Now we want to help him get his life back on course. He's a great artist and he should be working; that's when he's happiest."

Francisco had been told Rubens was close to Caravaggio, so he asked if he knew where he was, saying "We'll protect him again. He needs protection from himself as well as from Rome. You will be saving his life if you help us - the Church leaders in Rome want him dead." Rubens' court experiences had taught him never to take anyone's word in good faith. He'd learned there was usually another story lurking behind the one he was told. He knew Caravaggio's growing reputation was making his work valuable and suspected the Knights' motives were not simply designed to protect him.

His first reaction was to send word to Caravaggio's friend Mario Minitti asking for news. "Caravaggio is with me in Sicily, safe and working hard, but you know what he's like," Minitti wrote, "anything can happen with him. He goes his own way. What he really wants is to get back to Rome and be allowed to work again." Minitti wrote that Caravaggio had completed a work depicting The Burial of St Lucy, which he considered to be another masterpiece. Rubens knew the story of Lucy from the Book of Golden Legends, Legenda Aurea, written in the medieval period. Lucy was one of Sicily's most important saints, and Caravaggio had been paid much more than his usual fee. According to the story, Lucy had given all her wealth to the poor to show gratitude for the saving of her mother. "This is one of his finest works," Minitti wrote. "He's recreated her gentle spirit on canvas, giving her soft features and a pale face. Then he contrasts her still figure with the strong movement of the gravediggers." The painting had been commissioned by the Church of Santa Lucia al Sepolco in Syracuse. Lucy was wrongly accused by a suitor of infidelity. She refused to recant and offered her chastity to Christ but was sentenced to be dragged to a brothel. Miraculously, she could not be moved, so her throat was cut with a dagger.

She bled to death, and the church was built on the ground where she fell. Rubens felt that if the painting were as good as Minitti said, it would draw hundreds of pilgrims to the Church. Minitti had seen many of Caravaggio's paintings, so Rubens trusted his judgement and his judgement was proven correct. The crowds came, eager to see a picture that did justice to their saint. Later Minitti wrote that Caravaggio had painted another subject, The Raising of Lazarus, which was even more successful. It brought big crowds to the Church of Padri Crocifera in Messina. Rubens had grown certain that the Knights simply wanted Caravaggio back because his work attracted pilgrims to Malta and their churches. Malta was a small offshore island, and the presence of Caravaggio would bring cultural prestige to the Knights.

"These pilgrims bring gifts. Caravaggio makes money for them, it's as simple as that," Rubens wrote to his brother. He also informed Francisco that he'd tried and failed to trace Caravaggio. "That's a shame, I'll carry on searching," Francisco replied. "I've spread the word in Campo Marzio, close to where he lived. I'll pay a reward for anyone who can find him."

Rubens was alarmed when he heard that. He had a feeling that Francisco would stop at nothing to get his hands on Caravaggio, and he didn't trust him in any way. In 17th century Rome, corruption and nepotism were the twins who ruled the seething city. When Pope Paul V made his young nephew Scipione Borghese a Cardinal, he began a project that gave Rome a magnificent cultural legacy, made the family hugely rich - and gave Fillide Melandroni her first glimpse of power. One of her early lovers was the sculptor and architect Gian Lorenzo Bernini, a genius with a hot temper and a roving eye. He also had Scipione as a patron, a happy situation that made Bernini the chosen one when important commissions were handed out. There was nothing underhand about that: the Cardinal was a supreme talent spotter who favoured Caravaggio, Rubens and Raphael as well as Bernini, the architect of St Peter's Square. Pope Paul gave Scipione control of Vatican funds, and he proved to be a ruthless financial operator, so successful that the Borghese family gradually came to own a third of all land south of Rome.

The process was a revelation for Fillide who travelled with Bernini on 'working trips' he used as an excuse to escape from his wife. Borghese often insisted Bernini accompany him so they could talk about architecture as they travelled through the countryside. The trips opened her eyes to the injustice Caravaggio raged about. "Borghese was like some rich Emperor," she reported to him. "Any time he saw a village he liked, he bought it. He did it legally but for really cheap prices. He was so mean. His money came from tributes paid to the Pope, and a lot of people were happy to sell when he told them they'd be helping God's holy work. But if they turned him down, he said they weren't paying their taxes and that they'd have to sell for an even cheaper price."

Rent from the land found its way into the Borghese purse and gave the Cardinal enough income to indulge his real interests in a big way. He was obsessed with art and over the years built up a spectacular hoard of pictures. The Pope gave him one hundred and seven pictures he'd casually confiscated from the studio of Guiseppe Cesari, a leading artist who taught Caravaggio when he first arrived in Rome. Raphael's painting Deposition was forcibly removed from the Baglioni Church by Papal Order - then added to Borghese's collection. It sat alongside masterpieces by Titian - and Caravaggio. Borghese also obtained two of Caravaggio's best-known works, Sick Bacchus and Boy With A Basket Of Fruit, from the same unfortunate artist, Cesari.

The Cardinal couldn't simply confiscate paintings, so he demanded to buy all the work in his studio, including the Caravaggios, at an outrageously low price. Borghese thought it was an offer Cesari couldn't refuse, but he was still sore over the one hundred and seven paintings - and said "No". Borghese didn't send the heavy mob round: he simply had him arrested on a false charge. Cesari threw his hands in the air and said, "Of course dear Cardinal, my mistake, I accept your generous offer."

Caravaggio soon heard about Borghese's activities (the news quickly travelled to Sicily), but if he was ever to make his way back to Rome he would be dependent on patrons like him more than ever. In the past, Borghese had given him protection on the frequent occasions he was in trouble with the law. This protection didn't just involve his regular court appearances. Opponents sometimes succeeded in having his work rejected, complaining that it showed a lack of decorum. An early version of the Inspiration of Saint Matthew was turned down because the beloved saint had his legs crossed and his bare feet crudely exposed to the public. In the picture, Matthew is shown learning to write, and an angel is teaching him. This was Caravaggio's metaphor for the world learning the truth from God. He was happy to show Matthew as an ordinary person; it went with his mission to draw the Church closer to the people.

Authorities who came between him and that mission frustrated him constantly. His tirades against them reflected his deeply held beliefs and he clung to them. But as Fillide pointed out to him, some of his best work was deliberately provocative. A bent and downtrodden old man, for example, was cast as Saint Peter and crucified upside down. Yet Borghese stood by him. One of the contradictions of his character was that while he unscrupulously supported the Pope financially, he was also supportive of Caravaggio's work and secretly planned to bring him back to Rome. He wasn't the only one; Rubens had also begun to speculate how he could influence the courts, allowing Caravaggio to return.

In Naples, Cardinal Colonna was also seriously worrying about Caravaggio's future. The Colonna family considered that they owed a debt to Caravaggio's father and grandfather. As a matter of honour, they intended to repay by protecting the son who was orphaned at a young age. They'd heard disturbing news about the connections of the Tomassoni family. The father of Ranuccio was a Military General who'd worked his way into the Pope's inner circle. He was intent on revenge for the death of his son and knew there were plans to bring Caravaggio back to Rome. He'd secured the appointment of another son, Giovanni, as Capo of the district where Ranuccio was killed. Giovanni would have the power to arrest Caravaggio on sight, and the Colonnas were told, "If that happens, it's the end for him. He'll never be seen again." Many inspired artists suffer for their art, but Caravaggio was suffering for the life he led.

His arrest and imprisonment in Malta had been a nightmare. Minitti and some other friends managed to bribe his prison guards, and they let him escape. He made his way to a beach where he was told a boat would be waiting to take him to Sicily. But when he arrived the boat wasn't there, and his friends were nowhere to be seen. He'd been forced to hide in fields and live on foraged vegetables for three months, worrying all the time that the Knights would find him. Then, finally, his friends came for him, explaining that the Knights suspected them and that they were being watched all the time. "But we got word to Cardinal Colonna about what happened, and he warned them off. He told them he would send his guards from Naples if anything happened to you." This brought relief to Caravaggio but not a happy ending. He convinced himself his enemies were everywhere - that he'd never be safe. The torment in so much of his work came from his feelings of vulnerability. He slept in his clothes with his sword in his hand, even when he was safe in Sicily. He had bad feelings about the Knights of Malta. "Those ungrateful pigs in Malta. I gave them one of my greatest paintings; I signed it, and this is how they treat me," he told Minitti.

Eventually, his insecurity and paranoia became too much. He told Minitti "My old friend, believe me: I'll never be able to repay what you've done for me, but I can't stay. I feel I can be safe and work well in Naples. That's where I must go."

Minitti had been with Caravaggio in many of his wild moments and understood. He had his own explanation and believed nothing would ever change. "Caravaggio is addicted to danger; he looks for crisis. It's part of him and he can't work without it," he told Rubens when he came looking for him. "He craves that moment of panic, then afterwards he can't wait to start painting. Look at his best pictures, the life that's in them. Something is going to happen, and it will shock you. He's always on the edge."

But Minitti also felt that Naples wasn't the end of the line for Caravaggio. "His heart's in Rome, I'm sure of it." Later, Cardinal Colonna was to tell Rubens that he feared Caravaggio would never be safe in Rome, Malta or Sicily. That's why he was he was so happy to see him in Naples and desperately wanted him to stay.

Philip E. Rowson

"We should have killed him when we had him at the Scrofa"

Giovanni Tomassoni the newly appointed Capo of Rome's Campo Marzio was under pressure to avenge the killing of his brother, Ranuccio. "Remember: there's a widow and a three-year old daughter who have been deprived of a husband and a father, yet this man still goes free," said Federico Giugoli, brother of Ranuccio's widow, Lavinia. Giovanni was not pleased to be reproached like this. He expected more respect and usually received it. His reply was to the point: "I am dealing with it. The only thing I need from you is a still tongue. You were there when it happened and all you did was get in the way. You and your brother just added to the confusion and that's how he got away. Leave now or you'll be arrested!" Giugoli left; Giovanni in this mood was not a man to argue with. Besides, he accepted that there was truth in what he said.

Too many of them had crowded into the Scrofa Inn, Caravaggio's favourite bar. Giovanni had three guards, and two of his brothers with him. That would have been enough without the Giugoli brothers, but they insisted on joining in as they thought they were on a mission to avenge the family honour. The story Rubens heard originally wasn't far from the truth. One of Caravaggio's best friends, Onorio Longhi, had been with him. Fortunately for both of them, two soldiers, Petronio Troppa and Giancarlo Aldati had agreed to join as 'bodyguards'. They knew the danger of his ways and (in return for a good bottle of wine) offered to stick with him if trouble started. They were comrades in arms during their days in the Roman Legion and had seen plenty of bar fights. The night turned out to be a lot more significant than a bar fight, but even so, they kept their word. At first, the arguments between Ranuccio and Caravaggio were purely verbal, but eventually, the exchanges developed physically. The pushing and aggression moved out of the bar, and they tangled together amongst the tables in the street. Troppa and Aldati followed, sticking close to the angry artist. Ranuccio tripped up and fell, but he was so intent on making his point that he continued to insult Caravaggio while lying on the ground, shouting up at him that his wife had told him what a bad lover Caravaggio was. The impulsive, temperamental Ranuccio certainly didn't expect what happened next. Caravaggio drew his sword and slashed down, aiming, in revenge, for the groin. As the blood spurted and Ranuccio screamed, Giovanni leapt towards Caravaggio, but Petronio Troppa was quicker. He put himself between them and grabbed hold of Giovanni, pinning his arms. In a fury, the frustrated Capo got one arm free, pulled his dagger, and stabbed Troppa. The ex-legionnaire was battle-hardened and managed to hang on long enough to shout to Caravaggio, "Go! Run!" Now it was Aldati who took control, seizing Caravaggio by the throat. "Listen," he roared, shaking him. "Run for your life!" He dragged him away and pushed him down the street. Instinctively, Caravaggio ran off as self-preservation took over. The Capo finally pulled himself away from Troppa but next he had to deal with Aldati who, seeing his comrade on the floor bleeding, picked up a chair and crashed it over his head screaming "Ti Uccidero!" - I'll kill you - together with a string of obscene Legionnaire threats about what was going to happen next. The Capo was staggering, only half-conscious, but his brothers were reluctant to take on the angry soldier who had plenty of support amongst a growing crowd. Instead, they shouted threats, telling him to get out fast while he still could. What had started as a brawl was in danger of becoming a riot until more guards arrived and the spectators drifted home, the excitement over. Friends pulled Aldati away from the scene to save him from arrest. Ranuccio lay dying where he fell; the sword had cut an artery. Troppo's wound turned out not to be serious, but he was taken to court the next day, where he received a short sentence for 'causing a disturbance.'

A couple of days later, Giovanni sent an official summons to Onorio Longhi saying he wanted to speak to him because he was a witness to a murder and may be called upon to speak in court. A note attached to the summons read, "You will hear something to your advantage." Onorio was the son of Martino Longhi the Elder, the architect who first began work on the Milanese National Church in Rome, San Carlo al Corso, and the family had a high profile in Rome. Both father and son were friends of Caravaggio, and while his father was well respected, Onorio had a reputation as a rowdy party-goer, well known in the brothels, bars and courts of Rome. Unlike Caravaggio, he didn't wear a sword, but he often had a servant with him who carried his badges of rank. Like Caravaggio, he was quick to take offence. Temperamentally, the two were similar and known to confide in each other - which was why Tomassoni sent for him. He began by saying how much he regretted the whole affair. "Ranuccio was a hot-headed fool," he admitted. "I don't even know if Caravaggio was to blame for any of it. My brother was shouting about him sleeping with his wife, but I don't think he was interested in her at all. As for Ranuccio's daughter, I'm sure her father is the lawyer who worked for them. Now Lavinia wants to marry someone else and the lawyer's going to adopt the child. It's a stupid situation, and I must make it go away. We've lost Ranuccio; the courtesans who worked for him are broke and complaining. They'll make noise and cause trouble. It should never have happened."

Onorio wondered why Giovanni was talking to him like this. He'd been worried when he got the summons and was wary of the Capo's reputation as a devious tyrant. It got a bit clearer when he continued. "I just want the whole story to be over. Too many important people are getting interested. Some support Caravaggio and want him back in Rome so he can paint for them, others want him tried and executed for murder. Some cardinals hate his paintings so much they want him killed. Then there's the money - people are losing money. The drama is bad for business and everybody's looking at me."

'Yes, but that's your problem, not mine,' Onorio thought, 'when do I get the good news?'

What Tomassoni said was true enough. His district, the Campo Marzio, was Rome's red-light area. Pope Paul V had ordered all the courtesans of Rome to move there and stay there. It meant other areas were quieter, more respectable, but Marzio was now a constant, twenty-four-hour magnet for citizens looking for sex. As Capo of the district, Giovanni Tomassoni had responsibilities - and opportunities. He was able to observe the comings and goings of senators, Cardinals, businessmen and bankers. He hadn't been in the post for long but already saw how much money he could make in rent and commission - and simply for keeping information to himself. The threat of a whisper that revealed where a judge or senator was, or who he visited, was enough to make money change hands. In return, he had to keep control, make sure the streets were safe for citizens who wanted secrecy and a good time.

"It would go well for your family if you helped me," Tomassoni said, finally getting to the point, "Perhaps not so well if you didn't. You're a good friend of Caravaggio: a confidante. You saw what happened. It could easily have been an accident, and the Papal Curia says that's what it was. A genius was provoked, and a pimp died. Now it can be forgotten. This is the solemn word of the Holy Father. We've tried to contact Caravaggio to give him this good news but had no success. The great Flemish artist and diplomat, Peter Paul Rubens, who knows him well has been contacted. Rubens knows people all over the art world but even he doesn't know where Caravaggio can be found. That's what he told one of the Knights of Malta, a man called Paolo Francisco anyway. Francisco has been offering money to anyone who can find Caravaggio and tell him he's welcome back in Malta, but nobody has claimed the reward yet. "That's why I think someone like you - a close friend - is the best way forward. Help him and help me. Deliver the message, and remember it comes from the highest authorities in Rome. Those above me say he will be pardoned and protected. He should return."

Before Onorio could speak, Tomassoni went on to apply the pressure. "You were there, an innocent bystander. But if you choose not to help me, this story could go another way. You could be an accomplice in the murder of my brother, a member of the gang that attacked me and my guards. You are well known in this area. Maybe you are mixed up with some unsavoury people. Maybe they spread dirty stories. And as they say, stinking mud sticks, so no more church commissions." Tomassoni smiled and spread his arms wide. "But it won't come to that. When Caravaggio comes back, your family will be smiling. The biggest design commissions in Rome will come your way, and the family name will live forever in the beautiful churches and palaces you create. For you, Longhi - we open many doors. Your career will flourish."

Onorio was too clever to believe Tomassoni's promises completely, but he definitely believed the threats. He left, promising to "Search and search, I will find him."

First he knew he had to speak to his father.

Philip E. Rowson

"This is our chance - the Longhi family will make Rome even more beautiful"

Onorio's father, Martino the Elder, was now an old man, but he had a brilliant career to look back on. He'd designed many of Rome's finest private palaces, including the Palazzo Borghese. He created new buildings for the Vatican and owned three houses in the centre of Rome.

By nature, he was calm, dignified and professional - everything Onorio wasn't. The son was talented, educated and well-travelled, but also erratic, egotistical and bad tempered. In other words a mirror to Caravaggio, which was why they tolerated each other. It meant they didn't argue as much as they did with other people. Both were notorious as troublemakers.

"Pope Paul V will be at our right hand," Onorio told his father enthusiastically. "This is the moment that we create our own Baroque buildings here, in Rome. The Church needs to stay true to itself but move with the times. They need to lure the faithful back to Catholicism, away from that German Martin Luther and his dangerous Protestant ideas. They need beautiful buildings with authority. We'll give them inspiration - the spirit of la Bellissima Roma."

Onorio was exaggerating the opportunities but thinking about Longhi family traditions too. This was a moment of generational change. Everywhere in Rome, he saw architecture that was restrained, rational and geometric, much like his father's work. New attitudes meant that rules could be discarded. The walls of his palaces would curve in elegant shapes, staircases would become grand entrances. He'd use extravagant layering on exteriors to startle - then fascinate - the passeggiare. As his thoughts developed, he imagined cool interiors with dark shade, suddenly lit by shafts of chiaroscuro light. Striking colour schemes would announce the new, uniquely Longhi, Baroque. The rebel in Onorio couldn't wait to get started. He didn't spell out to his father that his time was over, he didn't want to upset him.

His father swiftly brought him back to reality, "Remember what you have to do first: Find Caravaggio and bring him back."

"Yes, and I'll do that. There's good reason why he must come back. The time is right for him. He has the vision, more than anyone, to take the Church to the people. He makes it real, unlocks the drama in the Bible stories. He'll be protected, and there are patrons waiting for him. We'll work together."

The idealist in Onorio was always at odds with his expeditions to Rome's underworld: his many disputes and court appearances. But both sides of his character were equally strong, and maybe, he thought, he could use the dark side to help his architectural ambitions.

That's why the next day, he was sitting with Fillide Mellandroni in rooms that were not so richly furnished as the ones he'd seen her in before. "With Ranuccio gone it's not so easy to find good clients," she shrugged. "Not that I miss him. Even though he's dead I have no good words for him, il Bastardo!"

Onorio quickly agreed with her. "His death caused many problems, but with your beauty, you'll survive. I can see why Caravaggio chose you to model for Catherine of Alexandria. She was loved for her beauty, fearlessness, intelligence . . . virginity. Well, three out of four isn't bad," he smiled. She accepted the joke and shot back, "Yes, but it will take more than flattery to get into my bed. That's what you want, isn't it? But it's not so easy."

She thought for a moment, "Caravaggio is a genius but a strange man... Made me sit still for hours for every picture, not moving. He said Catherine was a martyr, but so was I! Sometimes he didn't even pay me, and Cardinal del Monte paid him well. But Ranuccio hated him. He was jealous, he thought Caravaggio lay with me. And maybe he did, maybe he didn't. No one will know. I keep my secrets." Onorio saw his chance: "But perhaps there is one you could share with me - and I will pay you, very well. Important people want Caravaggio to come back to Rome and paint for them, and the Pope will pardon him for the killing of Ranuccio. He'll be protected; the Capo of Campo Marzio, Ranuccio's brother Giovanni, has been commanded to end this whole affair. The senior cardinals and the Pope want Caravaggio back where he belongs, in Rome, painting. Doing God's work."

Fillide listened to this, hardly believing what she was hearing. "What, Giovanni Tomassoni will protect the man who killed his brother?"

"Yes, because Ranuccio was a fool and big trouble for his brother. There is no grief for him. The only thing Giovanni wants is to carry on being Capo. It's a position that makes him rich and happy. He'll lose it if this Caravaggio problem isn't solved. All of Campo Marzio is in uproar over the killing, you know that. The Capo has to make everything normal again." The young Fillide was beginning to see where this might lead. She'd been a working girl since she was sixteen when her mother introduced her to the ways of Campo Marzio. Now, at twenty-two, she was streetwise and well aware of her power over men. "It's true what you say about Marzio: Giovanni has been losing out. He likes being rich and in charge, for sure. Where do I fit into this?" She had a good idea but enjoyed asking questions she already knew the answer to. It helped her decide who to believe - a vital decision in her dangerous trade.

Onorio knew he was entering a long negotiation, so began gently. "You were close to Caravaggio. I know because he told me. When people are close, they whisper to each other, sometimes on the pillow. Things they wouldn't say to other people. So, if he thought he was in danger of his life, where would he go? Who could he trust?" Fillide moved into business mode immediately. "Before we go any further, I need to see some coin, you know that. Get your money bag out and put two hundred scudi in my hand." He did as he was told, counting the money into her outstretched palm. "Right, so we begin," she said. "This must be important, or you wouldn't come here after all the trouble. That is just your first payment. Let's say, another fifty down the line, and I will begin to make arrangements. When there is a plan in place, you pay me the first instalment of five hundred, then a final five hundred when Caravaggio is back here in Rome. That's the way it has to be."

Onorio protested, "That's a lot when I don't know what I'm getting. I'll pay you five hundred when I see Caravaggio."

"Don't take me for a fool. You are desperate to find him, I can see that. Don't try to bargain with me, or you get nothing. It doesn't matter to me whether he comes back to Rome or not. Life will go on, and you have to solve your own problems. But with me, it's quicker; I know certain things. In any case, I have other rich people to deal with, so don't waste my time!" Fillide showed a flash of her famous temper. "Fine, fine, we can talk about the money," Onorio soothed her. "Here's another fifty for your time today, and we'll talk again soon. I think we both want to see him back in Rome." She pocketed the money and nodded, her mood softening.

"Let's do that. Now you can take me to cafe Sori for some wine." It was good for business for Fillide to be seen with someone of Onorio's standing. They both had some thinking to do. He'd made a start, but he wasn't sure whether Fillide could help him, and whether she would even if she could. She could be as erratic as the artist himself. In any case, the whole saga of Caravaggio's return was mixed up with deep divisions in the Catholic Church. Some were over theology and how to deal with the growing Protestant movement; would his realism help the Church to reach out to the people, or was he a danger to traditional Catholic teachings? Contrary to what Giovanni Tomassoni had boldly told Onorio, nobody could be sure where the Pope stood in the argument, least of all whether he would use the Vatican coffers to fund a new building programme.

Scipione Borghese, however, was trusted by the Pope to run Vatican finances, and he might well persuade his uncle that the right thing to do was buy from artists like Caravaggio instead of funding costly architecture.

Philip E. Rowson

Another opportunity for Fillide

Rumours about available cash quickly leapt from mouth to mouth in Campo Marzio. Fillide soon heard the story about Paolo Francesco and the reward the Knights of Malta were offering but didn't know anything about him or these Knights. Was it a devout religious order, or were they money-grabbing soldiers? She wasn't about to blunder into a situation without knowing some basic facts. This one had enough complications already; a wrong step was dangerous. The conversation with Onorio was intriguing, but on no account was she going to sell her friend out.

She was ready to deal with Onorio - cheat him and take his money if necessary - but she wasn't going to put Caravaggio in danger. He would jump at the chance to return to Rome, she was sure of that, and the idea that a Tomassoni was making it possible would make him laugh at life's absurdities. On the other hand, he might be happy and settled in new surroundings. Maybe his experiences had changed him, and he preferred to work where he was safe and appreciated. Yet she did warm to the idea of making some easy money from this unknown Knight. He was only a man; she could handle him. Caravaggio had confided to her, one drunken night, that he always had somewhere to run to. At first, he was reluctant to say, but Fillide knew how to get men to part with information. Eventually, a combination of ego and lust got the better of him, and he boasted, "I have a refuge, the Colonna family will protect me, they feel they owe me something because the plague took my father and grandfather while they were working for them. I will be safe in Naples but . . . I always feel that Rome is my home. It's where I work best." So, she could tell Onorio, after she'd coaxed as much cash as possible out of him.

She could give Francisco the same treatment. She just had to meet him and work out what kind of a man he was. He might not agree to see her. But then again, he might. In her experience men of the Church could be tempted. When she asked around, one of her friends told her everything she needed to know. "The Knights are powerful - some say as powerful as the Pope. And don't worry, they're definitely interested in women, especially when they're in Rome." Next came the information that convinced her, "Those that come are always rich."

It wasn't long before she crossed paths with Francisco. One afternoon she was drinking in Campo Marzio with Ranuccio Tomassoni's nephew Sandro, who wanted to take over as her pimp.

Normally, he would have aggressively moved in on any woman he thought might earn him money, but he was reluctant to make a move until he found out whether his uncle, Capo Giovanni, was interested in her. He'd never admit it, but he was also intimidated by her intelligence. So, for the moment, he was just trying to be helpful, protective if necessary.

Looking around the café for possible new customers, Fillide spotted a well-dressed man she'd never seen before and could tell from his accent that he wasn't from Rome. "Who's that over there," she asked Sandro. He didn't know but offered to ask if he wanted to join them for a drink. "Tell him I have been a model for the famous artist, Caravaggio," she said. "He might be someone I want to meet." She watched as Sandro went across and was delighted to see him get a quick reaction. The man's head jerked round, and he got to his feet immediately. Arriving at her table he smiled and said, "I've admired your pictures, now I see you in the flesh. May I sit down? I'd like to talk to you about Caravaggio. What a talent the man has."

"Well, he has good material to work with, here in Rome," she smiled, complimenting herself. Turning to Sandro, she introduced him, "This is Sandro Tomassoni, nephew of the Capo of San Marco, Giovanni Tomassoni." Sandro had served his purpose, showing that she was close to authority in the community and she no longer wanted him involved in the conversation. "Thank you, Sandro, I'll see you again soon."

She dismissed him with a beaming smile that made his heart jump - she was a beautiful woman. Taking the hint, he bowed briefly to Francisco and left. "I am Paolo Francisco, a member of the Knights of Malta," he announced, sitting down. "Caravaggio came to Malta and painted one of the world's great masterpieces for us, The Beheading of St John the Baptist. Cruel but so real. An incredible piece of work, truly one of the great altarpieces. We are privileged to have it in St John's Cathedral in Malta. Crowds come to see it, many from Rome. They stay and marvel."

"I can understand that," Fillide said. "No one can capture a scene like the great Caravaggio. I, too, am privileged that he's chosen me for so many paintings. It's so wrong that he's been driven from Rome. He killed someone because he was challenged and insulted. The person he killed deserved to die." Fillide spoke fiercely but didn't tell him she was involved with Ranuccio. She wanted to gauge his reaction to her outburst, but he was too excited about meeting her. "What a lucky day for me," he exclaimed. "I meet a beautiful woman, then discover she knows Caravaggio well. First, let me say, the Knights of Malta share your feelings about his talents. We want him back with us, continuing his great work." He kept to himself the way they'd imprisoned him. Anyway, he thought, how would she know? "We'll pay a handsome reward to anyone who can find him and help us to bring him back to Rome."

"Really?" Fillide acted surprised. "That's very generous, but I think it will be difficult. As everyone says, he's a man who goes his own way." Then, she decided to go in hard - he seemed like a serious man. "At least a thousand scudi will be needed." Francisco didn't blink, he realised he was talking to someone well used to negotiation. "So, you know where he is. Are you sure? I've asked many others, and nobody seems to know."

"That's because you haven't been asking the right people. I can find out in two days, maybe sooner," Fillide replied, "but nobody will speak without money. Caravaggio knows important people who will hide him." They carried on talking, and Fillide managed to persuade him to part with fifty scudi upfront. "Perhaps I will come to know you better as we talk about this," he said, suggestively, as he was leaving. "Possibly," she smiled. "First I have to find the right people and talk to them."

She had one important contact she'd never used before but now was the time. Cardinal Baronius was a member of the influential College of Cardinals and a trusted confidante of the Pope. He was also someone who'd been close to Fillide's mother in her working days, and a frequent visitor to their home. He'd known her as a child, and when she sent him a message, he agreed to see her. They met discreetly in the Church of Sant'Anna dei Palafrenieri, close to the Vatican. Dressing modestly and wearing a veil, she waited at the back of the church until a priest took her to a small private chapel. "Thank you for seeing me, your Eminence," she started, bending to kiss his hand. "Forgive me for disturbing you, but I come with a message that only someone as important as yourself can deliver, and it relates to the Holy Father's wishes. The message is for the artist Caravaggio, who I think is being protected by Cardinal Colonna in Naples."

She paused, waiting for a reaction, and when he nodded, she continued. "The message is that his friend, Onorio Longhi the architect, will visit him soon and bring him back to Rome. Longhi will say that he believes Pope Paul will pardon him, that it is safe to return, and that Cardinal Borghese wishes him to continue the Church's work in Rome." Cardinal Baronius listened carefully and thought for a moment, then spoke.

"This is possibly true. I cannot speak for the Holy Father or Cardinal Borghese, but the message will be delivered to Caravaggio." Fillide thanked him, kissing his proffered hand again. "Give my greetings to your mother, Fillide," he said. "And take care in Campo Marzio; these are dangerous times."

"Make your home here; we'll make your studio here…"

Peter Paul Rubens tries to persuade Caravaggio to stay in Naples

After talking to Minitti, Rubens knew he had to travel to Naples and warn Caravaggio about the dangers of a return to Rome. They were sitting in Caravaggio's favourite tavern as the sun slowly faded, casting shadows between the tables. They'd been talking for two hours about mutual friends and news from Rome while the noise of other conversations flowed around them. Rubens gradually turned the conversation to the blessings of life and work in Naples, as opposed to the distractions and dangers of Rome. He gestured around the room; in the growing darkness a cast of faces shone as candles were lit. "See, the light comes and goes, just the way it does in Rome. The sights that tempt you to paint are here: ordinary people with their life's work written on their bodies and faces. There are people here who understand art: patrons with big purses who want to commission your work. Think about this too: you're safe here because Cardinal Colonna has people everywhere and he's given them a duty - a duty to look after you even when you get excited and argue like a wild man. I know that because he's told me personally - and Cardinal Colonna does not lie. You have good friends here. My strong advice," Rubens paused, put a hand on Caravaggio's arm as it rested on the table, wanting the words to sink in, "is choose life in Naples, my friend, not disaster in Rome. You have so much to give to the world; nobody can paint like you." There was a pause as Caravaggio considered. He was moved by the generous words. "Ah Rubens, you speak nearly as well as you paint. I see why kings and queens ask to consult with you in the courts of Europe. I am honoured, and because you have travelled here to talk to me, I must give you an honest answer. I want to return to Rome to work, and in the coming days, I am expecting to hear some good news: there is a strong rumour that the Pope has pardoned me for the Tomassoni affair. I've received a message informing me that my friend Onorio, the architect, is coming here to Naples. He will give me news of the pardon and talk about the paintings the Church needs in Rome. They have big plans for a counter reformation; these are exciting times, and I can be a part of it."

Rubens was hugely disappointed, but he wasn't going to give up, especially when he heard that Onorio was involved. He'd met him several times in Rome and thought he was too similar in his ways and mindset to Caravaggio to be a stable advisor - or even a reliable source of information. "Onorio, really? I know he's a good friend, but I don't think the Pope would use him to deliver important messages. The last time I saw him he was drunk in a café in Campo Marzio, being spoken to by the Papal guard for bad behaviour. How can he compare to Cardinal Colonna?" Caravaggio laughed, "I would never compare him to the Cardinal who is a good friend and a good man. But times change, and Onorio has been summoned by the Capo of Campo Marzio. He told Onorio that he had been ordered by Pope Paul V to protect me when I return. Onorio says the Pope wants new art and new buildings to turn the eyes of the people away from the Protestants. We'll work together. This is good for me, please try and be happy for me."

Rubens was getting worried now. If true, it was sweet news for Caravaggio - but he was sure it wasn't. He'd heard rumours of new thinking in the Vatican and worries about the rise of Protestant thinking, so it sounded plausible, but he wasn't convinced. "Of course, I'd be happy for you if I could be sure it was true. But you have many dangerous enemies in Rome. The Capo of Campo Marzio is Giovanni Tomassoni, the brother of Ranuccio!"

"I know that, but as I said, times change," Caravaggio was speaking seriously now. "Giovanni knows Ranuccio was a fool, a danger to himself and everyone around him. So, he will do as the Pope says, and I have friends as well as enemies in Rome.

The Pope's nephew, Cardinal Scipione Borghese, has commissions for me. I have to take this work when it is offered; nobody knows what happens next, do they, my friend?"

Rubens didn't answer for a moment. He could see Caravaggio's mind was made up. "I'm afraid for you, afraid that you're making a big mistake. But if I can't change your mind, then I wish you well." He knew some of what his fellow artist was saying was true: there would be commissions from Borghese. "I will visit you in Rome, and I hope you can continue your work."

The day after her conversations with Francisco and Cardinal Baronius, Fillide put the first part of her plan to extract money from the Caravaggio situation into action. She summoned Onorio and told him she knew where the painter was. "So, this is where you get your money bags out. I want five hundred scudi for the information now and another five hundred when he's back in Rome. Don't try to trick me or bargain with me, or you will be found lying in the gutter not far from here. You know I have many friends in Campo Marzio who will be pleased to give you a beating." This was a different Fillide to the smiling courtesan he usually saw, and he knew she could easily hire someone to do what she said.

The streetwise woman had taken charge. He didn't try to haggle with her and counted five hundred into her hand. "He's in Naples guarded by

Cardinal Colonna, and very soon I'll arrange for somebody to travel with you to see him. It could be dangerous, I'll arrange bodyguards. Caravaggio is a difficult man, and he has enemies who don't want him back in Rome. There's a boat from Porto Ecole, just up the coast from Naples, and it will bring you straight here, to Rome. I'm arranging all this for you so that there won't be any mistakes and he'll be kept safe. Believe me, this is a bargain I'm giving you." In truth, she needed to control the situation so that she could collect from Francisco too, but all Onorio could see was that she was making it easier for him. He couldn't organise it himself, and only the day before, Capo Giovanni had sent messages to remind him what was required.

"Don't worry, everything will go well," Fillide assured him, "and we'll be serving the Holy Father who wants him back." Onorio was surprised to hear her bringing the Pope into the situation so directly, but that was good news. He knew she was more than friendly with certain Cardinals who were regular visitors to Campo Marzio. If the Pope's inner circle knew what was going on and approved, so much the better. Thinking about her plans later, Fillide decided to involve Sandro Tomassoni. She thought it might be a good idea to send him with Onorio. He was young but not inexperienced and, as a member of the Tomassoni family, no stranger to violence or the ways of the Roman underworld. She guessed he had the strength and personality to put some backbone into Onorio if he started to waver, and she'd choose the muscle to go with them. She was also getting to know him better. He was increasingly attentive and, she suspected, falling for her charms in a big way. That always helped, and if the plans worked out, she'd reward him with an afternoon in her bed. Mixing pleasure with business was never a problem. After she'd told him what was being planned, she continued, "This is a big opportunity for you, Sandro. Your uncle Capo Giovanni will be watching, and we need to get it right. The plan works for both of us, but it will be bad if it goes wrong. If you have any worries about whether you can do this, speak now. I won't think any less of you." She took his hand and looked into his eyes. Her life experience had made her a shrewd judge of character, and if she saw a flicker of doubt, she'd ask someone else. But he reacted the way she had hoped he might.

"I can do it," he said straight away. "I know Naples, and I have contacts with the Camorra. I know my way around. I can handle this. We'll bring Caravaggio back, don't worry." 'Yes!' she thought to herself. "He is a Tomassoni, but I trust him the way I never trusted Ranuccio, and his contacts with the Mafia in Naples could be vital.' But first, she had to convince a suspicious Knight of Malta that she could deliver Caravaggio.

She sent a message inviting him to meet her in her apartment in Campo Marzio to hear about the missing artist. "I've made enquiries about him, asking people who have to be paid for their information," she said, underlining that money was now owed. "There are rumours he's been hiding in many places: Sicily, Tuscany, the Greek Islands," she'd made the last two up, but who was to know? "Before I say where you'll find him, you have to put cash on the table." Francisco paused for a moment. He was a senior Knight of Malta, an order some said was equal to the Pope, and this woman from the streets of Rome was demanding money from him. "If we were somewhere else," he began, "I'd tell someone to beat it out of you. I might still do that; Rome is a violent place, and no one will miss a whore from Campo Marzio."

That kind of talk wouldn't get him anywhere with Fillide Melandroni: this was street bargaining. She didn't hesitate and changed her tone dramatically. "You're a fool to even think that," she shouted at full volume. "If I go to the window and call out, see what happens. Men will come running, and you'll be cut to pieces where you stand." She was openly contemptuous now. "What sort of behaviour is this from a man of the cloth?" She edged closer to the table where she kept a knife, fastened to the underside. She'd used it once before when she feared for her life. "If you haven't brought any money, leave now and we'll forget all about it." Casually she sat down at the table and put one hand on the knife fixed underneath. Francisco had no intention of carrying out his threat. Knights of Malta had no status in Rome. He wasn't carrying a sword, and he knew Fillide would have a pimp close by. Maybe that youth who was with her in the café? But there would be many others ready to protect Fillide from an outsider. So, he simply said, "How will I know what you tell me is true? You could be feeding me lies."

"That's a risk you take. One thousand scudi on the table now or leave and forget it. But no one else will help: the Knights aren't liked here." It was maddening, but Francisco knew it was true. If Caravaggio was welcomed back to Rome, they'd never persuade him to leave and return to Malta. "Five hundred scudi now, and another five hundred when he's back with us," he offered. She thought for a brief moment, "Put seven hundred and fifty down now and we'll forget the other two hundred and fifty," she said. "Take it or leave it."

"I'll take it - and now you can take your hand off that knife under the table. I know how you do business in Campo Marzio." He counted the money onto the table and stood back. After all, he reasoned, if he didn't like what he heard, he could return with some troops of his own, or catch her unawares outside Campo Marzio. "So, speak to me."

"Caravaggio is in Naples, where he's protected by Cardinal Colonna," Fillide was relaxed now. She knew she'd won, and she'd teach him not to threaten a woman of the Marzio. "You'll never reach him there; the Cardinal protects him like a son. So, what we have to do is lure him away from

Naples." Francisco was listening closely now; he'd long suspected Caravaggio was with the Colonna family and the Knights had a historic feud with them. He'd get no help there. "Caravaggio is desperate for a pardon so he can come back and work in Rome," she continued. "There's so much work for him here. A message, bearing a seal from the Pope's nephew Cardinal Borghese, has been sent to him saying the Pope has pardoned him. He's free to come back and work. The man who sent the message is one of Caravaggio's closest friends, and he was with him on the night he carried out the murder. He'll be leaving in three weeks to travel to Naples to bring Caravaggio back."

She could see Francisco was about to interrupt, but she held her hand up, "I know what you're going to say, so wait. Cardinal Colonna doesn't want him to leave Naples: he doesn't trust Rome. So, Caravaggio's going to leave quietly with a friend and travel to Porto Ecole up the coast. From there, he'll take a boat to Rome. That's the plan. The boat sails on the twenty-fifth day of June, and they'll leave Naples to catch it on the twenty-second. What you have to do, is stop them on the road just outside Porto Ercole on the twenty fourth and take Caravaggio to Malta - not Rome. Today, we're at the beginning of June, so you have more than enough time to make arrangements. You can sail from Porto Ercole to Malta." Francesco was taking his time, thinking this through. "Tell me, who are the people who will be with Caravaggio? His friend, and who else?"

"Just two servants who will carry Caravaggio's paints, brushes and canvases. His work always goes with him," she answered, beginning to guess what the next question would be. "What if Caravaggio insists on travelling to Rome?" he asked. She'd been right. "That's up to you. He's worked for you before, why shouldn't he again? I've told you what we agreed, where you can find him. Now it's up to you. If you offer him enough, he'll work for you. If he argues, take some men with you, and force him. You aren't afraid of violence, are you?" she ended, mocking him. "But don't think of trying to take him from Naples, because Colonna's men will arrest you and throw you in prison for a long time. Just remember the dates. Caravaggio will be approaching Porto Ercole on the twenty-fourth of June."

"I hope for both our sakes you're telling the truth," he said seriously. "How do you know this, anyway?" "I'm from Campo Marzio: it's my business to know what's happening. I've done you this service, and you've paid me. I wish you success. I don't want any harm to come to Caravaggio, so be careful, or you will answer to many people in Rome and Naples. He can be as great a painter in Malta as he is in Rome."

Francesco could see there was nothing more to be said, as far as she was concerned. He didn't really trust her, but he knew this was the best chance of finding Caravaggio, and he was already planning to get together a troop of soldiers to 'persuade' Caravaggio to come with him. "Perhaps when he is working with us in Malta, I could visit you again and we can enjoy a better conversation - or maybe more?"

"We'll see what life delivers to us," she laughed. She judged each day based on how much money she earned, and today she'd earned plenty. She'd also helped to keep Caravaggio safe, and that was important to her. She certainly didn't believe Francesco had the artist's best interests at heart. Despite the trouble Caravaggio so often brought to anyone he encountered, she sincerely hoped to see him back in Campo Marzio soon. In her opinion, he added prestige to her hunting ground. He was an attraction, a celebrity, a talent - which meant rich people would come to see him, and she'd be happy to entertain them: usually in her bed. As to what might happen when Francesco realised he'd been tricked, she was relaxed. There could be many explanations why he hadn't intercepted Caravaggio in Porto Ercole, and she'd be happy to provide them - for a fair price, of course.

Onorio Longhi suggested to Fillide that they should take the two soldiers, Troppa and Aldati, with them to Naples. "They saved Caravaggio that night. They were brave and he knows them." She hadn't yet told him that Sandro would be going with him and how that might cause complications because of the way they'd attacked the Capo. Even so, it could work out well, so she simply said, "Leave it with me, I'll check them out." When she put the idea to Sandro, he laughed out loud. "You mean the two who nearly killed the Capo?" He'd heard all about the night from friends who were there. "They were good. Two legionnaires who just jumped in after Caravaggio stabbed Ranuccio. A good job they did: Giovanni would have killed him, but they stopped him. They're tough." What appealed most to Fillide was that Caravaggio knew them and what they'd done, all for a bottle of wine. "The Capo doesn't have to know anything about this. All he's interested in is getting him back. Caravaggio can be impossible, but when he sees them, I think he'll relax. He'll trust them, and Onorio can tell him everything's going to work out fine, that there's going to be lots of commissions for him. Then, when you say you've got a message from the Capo " –

"That he's going to kill him as soon as he sees him!" Sandro interrupted her, but he was laughing. Noticing her expression, he quickly said, "That's just a joke. I'll tell him everything's changed, Giovanni's been told he has to protect him."

Fillide kept her stern look. "I'll forget you said that. Don't behave like a foolish boy, or I might change my mind about you." Inwardly she smiled; she liked Sandro's spirit. "Go and talk with the Legionnaires," she told him. "Don't tell them everything. Just say we need an escort for a trip to Naples and back, and they'll be well paid. Whatever you do, don't mention Caravaggio's name 'til you've left Rome - and don't tell them you're the Capo's nephew." Onorio didn't object when Fillide told him Sandro would be going with him as well as the soldiers. He saw it as another example of the way her mind worked. Sandro was there to make sure he didn't get any ideas about working out an alternative plan with Caravaggio; it meant she didn't really trust him. Well, the feeling was mutual, but all he wanted was Caravaggio back in Rome and ready to collaborate with him. Fillide told them to leave immediately.

Troppa and Aldati were happy to go along with what sounded like a routine escort job and the pay was generous. When they saw Onorio, they quickly worked out what might be involved but said nothing. They were foot soldiers, ready to take orders to earn their keep.

Philip E. Rowson

"I am not yet inclined to live the life of a celibate"

Peter Paul Rubens in a letter to a friend shortly after his second marriage

Realising that Caravaggio was determined to return to Rome and that there was nothing more he could do, Rubens decided to return to Antwerp and pick up his career there. He built a family home in the style of an Italian Renaissance Palace and was appointed Court Painter by Archduke Albert and the Infanta Isabella, joint rulers of the Netherlands on behalf of Catholic Spain. Rubens had been raised as a Catholic, but in his work had never felt the need to stick to the strict formality of the Church. Throughout his life, his work displayed a powerful lust for life, and he painted many female nudes. After he was widowed, he married a shapely, sixteen-year-old blonde who he felt 'Would not blush when he picked up his brushes to show off her naked splendour.'

He combined his earthly tastes with a philosophical outlook that was deeply anti-war, working for years to bring the royal houses of

Europe together and end the disastrous thirty-year conflicts responsible for millions of casualties. Rubens had short-lived successes and was highly respected for his skills in diplomacy, but many national leaders followed the code of Machiavelli that said, "Nothing brings a prince more prestige than great campaigns," and, "Audacity is always better than caution."

Rightly or wrongly, the Flemish master became best known as an exponent of the sensuous Baroque style, particularly in his portrayal of women. Stick-thin models were not to be found in his studio. In this period, the ideal woman was generously full-figured and was painted so by Rubens. So distinctive was this style that hundreds of years later whenever the term 'Rubenesque' was used, it quickly brought to mind an image. His painting *Venus In Front of the Mirror* was typical of his style, both idyllic and realistic: a luxurious, majestic expression of womanhood. Rubens used the mirror to convey the thought that the image was so real it could be compared with the real thing as seen in flesh and blood. Her skin is soft and delicate, her hair silky. A single, jewelled arm bracelet draws attention to her nakedness. The figure of Cupid holds the mirror and is deliberately in her shadow. The framing around the mirror and the figure of a maidservant combine to create a dark background, emphasising Venus's glowing figure and confident, seductive half-smile. The work added to Rubens's growing fame.

His studio employed many artists and apprentices: he was a shrewd judge of what would sell and became increasingly wealthy. His focus on archetypal female roles, from wives and widows to diplomatic regents, raised the status of his subjects, and he became an image-maker for sophisticated women. The Queen Mother of France, Maria de' Medici, commissioned him to paint a series of twenty-four pictures celebrating her life and times - a commission that was both grand and delicate. Maria had ruled as regent on behalf of her eight-year-old son, King Louis XIII until he was fifteen. Soon after his ascension, he exiled her. She wasn't allowed to return to Paris for four years, and the bad blood between them continued until her death. The commission tested Rubens' diplomatic skills: he had to do justice to Maria without offending the King. He succeeded by producing extravagant portraits of her surrounded by ancient, respected but non-threatening gods. He made her a personification of a glorious France, appearing as a heroic, bare-breasted figure. It was a Tour de Force by the Flemish master. The paintings brought her prestige without challenging the King, a typically subtle Rubens ploy.

Unsurprisingly the series attracted the attention of leading Cardinals close to Pope Paul V. Principal among them was Cardinal Priest Maffeo Barberini, an ambitious man who had plans to one day become Pope. Barberini was an ally of Cardinal Borghese: they shared some of the same cultural interests, and he was impressed by the work that the architect Gian Lorenzo Bernini had carried out for Borghese. "Maybe we should think about using the talents of this Rubens," he told Bernini. "He has a tactical gift for satisfying people who come from different sides." Bernini's reputation was already made, but he knew patrons could be fickle, so he was eager to agree with the man everyone expected to be the next Pope.

"We can use that kind of talent," he said. "There'll be difficult days ahead." Bernini's vision extended from dramatic architecture to sculpture and painting, and he could create the kind of singular, dominant impression that Barberini was looking for when he eventually became Pope Urban VIII.

The new Pope was determined to create a spectacular, all-powerful Rome that would outshine and outlast the new Protestant thinking. For him, Rome wasn't just a city, it was the expression of an all-powerful faith. He wanted to literally rebuild that faith, and Bernini had done much to impress him. His work at St Peter's with a four-pillared, gilded bronze canopy that rose ninety-eight feet from the ground produced a startling, theatrical effect never seen before in any of the great European cities.

Bernini appreciated the work of Rubens but did have his reservations. As far as he was concerned, Caravaggio was his natural collaborator.

He took the Pope to see The Calling of St Matthew and explained how Caravaggio worked. "See the drama he creates by shadowing the face of Christ but highlighting the face of Matthew. It's the light of revelation, there on the canvas. And he uses colours you see every day, he paints the kind of people you see every day, so you recognise the scene. He uses light to show you how you should be looking at the picture to get the most out of it. Then you come back to take in the detail and the story is all there, clearer than in one of your long sermons," he laughed.

The Pope enjoyed his 'lesson,' but he also knew every Pope had to make compromises at some time, and he didn't forget Rubens. There was another reason why Bernini favoured Caravaggio. Namely, he was suspicious of Rubens' entrepreneurial attitudes. "He's more interested in making money than making great art. His studio is like a factory with workers who toil away, uninspired, like common labourers while Rubens collects commissions from royal courts and wealthy patrons all over Europe. We need a special look for Rome, one that springs from our Roman soul." This was powerful rhetoric, exactly what the Pope wanted to hear and Bernini went on to force his point home.

"The roots of Rubens are half a continent away in a cold climate. Caravaggio has some madness about him, but his eyes are Roman, and he's gifted like nobody else."

Bernini's judgement of Rubens was harsh and self-serving. He had his own plans to revitalise the look of Rome: to bring back a glory that would last for centuries and reflect on him alone. He wasn't looking for competition. His ideas - mixing sudden light sources with mysterious chiaroscuro effects - would work seamlessly alongside Caravaggio's art. He saw the mercurial, erratic painter working harmoniously alongside him; there was no room for Rubens. Three would be a crowd.

At that moment, Caravaggio was on a boat carrying him back to Rome. He'd been delighted to see Onorio arrive and made him repeat every detail of what he'd heard about his return and pardon. Onorio reassured him again, "Cardinal Baronius who sits at the right hand of the Pope arranged for that message to be sent to you. It means you will be pardoned; you'll be safe and commissions will be waiting for you. Good times are on the way for Rome, and we'll be part of them." "And who is this, what's his part?" Caravaggio demanded next, looking fiercely at Sandro.

"I'm here, like Onorio, to pledge that you will be safe," Sandro answered directly. "My uncle is Capo of Campo Marzio, and he's been instructed to keep you safe when you return. He told me to tell you he's investigated what happened on that night with Ranuccio and has reported to the city authorities that you were attacked first. Cardinal Scipione Borghese met with him to say he had important work for you, and it was the Capo's duty to protect you." Sandro had never had any such conversation with his uncle, but, together with Fillide, he'd worked out what to say to the volatile artist – who reacted cynically.

"So, the artist Capo is now a patron of the arts who wants nothing more than to save Caravaggio?" was the next question, delivered with a sneer. Onorio could see which way this was going and jumped in to support Sandro. "Amico Mio, if Giovanni wants to stay Capo - and he does, very much - he has to protect you." Eventually, Caravaggio was satisfied although he did warn Sandro, "I will be watching you, and all your family." When all was finally settled, he insisted on giving Troppa and Aldati money and wine, plus an introduction to the Madame of the finest brothel in Naples. "Comrades, it's the least I can offer. Without you I would not be here; the Capo was ready to slice me open like a pig on feast day. I have thanked you in my mind and my bones, many times."

One week later, Paolo Francesco was in a vastly different frame of mind. The Knight of Malta had been waiting with six soldiers on the road outside Porto Ecole to intercept Caravaggio and take him back to Malta. After three days, he was certain he'd been tricked by Fillide Mellandroni. "I should have known better than to trust a whore from Campo Marzio," he complained bitterly. He continued to Naples and was told that Caravaggio had left with three others. "I've lost a good customer," a tavern keeper told him. "He'll be in Rome now. They had a party here before they left. Caravaggio was celebrating - he was crazy, like always."

A new Pope arrives, and a new age begins

After the death of Pope Paul V, Pope Urban VIII, the most influential Pope of the period, was elected. He came into office with a reputation as a military leader and a great patron of the arts. This energetic, ambitious Pope was successful on both counts. He expanded the Papal States using political intrigue and military might while at the same time supporting his friend Gian Lorenzo Bernini as he transformed and rebuilt many areas of Rome, making the city the envy of Europe. He also increased the wealth of his family to an estimated one hundred and five million scudi, then elevated his brother and two nephews within the Papal hierarchy, making them all Cardinals. Popes like Urban VIII had real power and used it ruthlessly. When the Spanish faction of the College of Cardinals tried to have him arrested, he disbanded the College and ordered all cardinals to return to their churches. A significant cause of their unrest was the debt created by Urban that increased by thirty million scudi over his reign. He used the money to support Bernini's inspired ideas for renewal, such as the piazza leading to St Peter's which survives today. Bernini used rows of towering, semi-circular colonnades to create a space in the shape of an oval that allowed thousands of pilgrims to greet the Pope as he appeared on a balcony. The space echoed the salute of the Holy Father as he spread his arms wide, offering an exhilarating and expansive welcome that never failed to bring rousing cheers from the crowd.

This was political as well as spiritual image building that strengthened the power of the Pope in Rome at a time when it was under constant threat. Giovanni Tomassoni hadn't been exaggerating when he told Onorio Longhi there would be funds and commissions for rebuilding. Where he did totally mislead him was to promise that the opportunities would come the way of his family: they weren't his to offer. He was simply the Capo of one red-light district, important enough, but trivial beside the power Bernini now had. In some ways, the architect was as ruthless as his mentor. When his mistress was unfaithful to him with his brother, he flew into a wild rage and ordered one of his servants to go to Campo Marzio and beat her badly. The truth soon came out, but under Rome's corrupt justice system it was the servant that went to prison, and nothing was said about Bernini's role. The architect was a contradiction: a visionary with a narcissistic personality. His mistress was discarded forever, together with Onorio.

The young architect was hoping that the story of how he'd brought Caravaggio back to Rome would help to win him commissions – but Bernini didn't work that way. "I'm pleased Caravaggio is back alongside me," he said, "but there won't be any restoration commissions for you, Onorio. Rome needs a single vision, a vision that can make the whole city richer in every way. I have been trusted with this work by the Holy Father, and I intend to carry out my vision." Onorio pleaded his case, but Bernini was scornful. "Your father did some good work, but I've seen nothing from you. If you feel the Capo cheated you, go back to him. Maybe he'll commission a new brothel - that would be more suitable for you." It was a scathing rejection, unnecessarily insulting, but Onorio dare not answer back. Bernini's treatment of his mistress had shown all of Rome he was not a man to be crossed. The best he could hope for was a change in the thinking of the Vatican or, more happily for him, the downfall of Bernini.

Caravaggio was sympathetic. He understood the whims of patrons, but that was the life of an artist. "I talk with Bernini, and he lets me go my own way, which is all I ask. He only thinks of himself but what I do pleases him. Maybe something will happen to him in the future, who knows?"

"I'll be working to make something happen," Onorio thought, darkly. Fillide felt sorry for him. She'd earned well from the whole episode, and

Onorio had carried out his part. She definitely wasn't about to offer him a refund, but she could give him a gift in kind. "Come up to my apartment, bring a bottle of wine, and we'll spend some time together." That brought a smile to his face and as he was leaving, she gave him some advice. "Be patient, don't give up. I know this Bernini well, and he isn't a good person, anyone can see that. Something will happen to him one day, and he won't be the big man making decisions. Rome can be a bad place for people like him. I'll listen, and if I hear anything I'll tell you."

Since the success of the Caravaggio affair, she'd come to an arrangement with Sandro, although she didn't need a pimp anymore. She had a circle of wealthy admirers who took care of her financially, but Sandro was always on hand to offer protection and support. In return, she shared her bed with him regularly, and the situation gave him some prestige. He was still infatuated with her and recognised she was an intelligent woman with powerful friends. Enemies too, but that was inevitable in Campo Marzio. His uncle, the Capo, was a much happier man lately. With Caravaggio back at work the heat was off him, and business returned to normal. The usual mixture of extortion and corruption kept his income flowing; he was happy to look the other way when important people misbehaved in the Campo. If Bernini was the man chosen to plan the new Rome, that was fine by him; if another voice was in favour, that was fine too. He knew there would be disagreements over the millions of scudi being spent on new buildings and new artworks. All he had to do was listen to the voices surrounding the Pope and be ready to change allegiances if necessary.

Caravaggio was working on Bernini's chapel for the Cornaro family - one of the richest and most influential in Rome. The inspired baroque chapel is one of Bernini's most spectacular creations, theatrical and dramatic. In an echo of Caravaggio's Chiaroscuro, he used hidden light sources to pick out twenty different colours of marble. A triangular pediment suspended above the altar added depth to the building. Clouds and angelic figures on the ceiling inspired worshippers. Yet a centrepiece featuring a sculpture of The Ecstasy of Saint Teresa brought a more worldly dimension. A cupid figure pierces her with a flaming arrow, and her enjoyment of the sensation gave the work an erotic feeling.

The feeling of unease that the work of Caravaggio and Bernini brought to conservative thinkers inside the Vatican was highlighted by Caravaggio's altarpiece, The Martyrdom of Saint Ursula. It illustrated an ancient legend in which the Saint was on a pilgrimage to Rome but stopped over in Cologne with her eleven thousand virgin followers. The city was under siege by barbarians, the chief of whom was besotted by Ursula. When she resisted his advances, he killed her with an arrow and ordered the execution of her followers for refusing to have sex with his men. This emphasis on physical erotica in a religious setting was too much for some members of the College of Cardinals, who took their complaints to the Pope. "It's blasphemy by Bernini: blasphemy that distracts the people when they should be having heavenly thoughts. And who is working by his side? The murderer Caravaggio! This has to stop."

As he listened to their anger, the Pope remembered his conversation with Bernini about Peter Paul Rubens. His instinct was right; to succeed, they needed an artist who would work to chart a course between both sides of difficult arguments. There was no denying Rubens' stature as a Renaissance artist, so if Bernini wouldn't work with him, there were other talented architects who would. He admired the vision of Bernini, but, faced by a divided group of Cardinals, this was what he had to do. Soon after his decision, he summoned Cardinal Baronius, who hadn't been amongst the protesters. Baronius was a man he trusted to be discreet (although he didn't know about his connections to Campo Marzio). "I want you to take a message to the Flemish artist Rubens; he has certain qualities we need. He is an artist and a diplomat, and his diplomacy means he's succeeded where many have failed. Tell him there's an opportunity to work on the greatest project of our age: the rebuilding of Rome, and that he will be well rewarded - be sure to emphasise that. I want him to work with Bernini. To make progress, we need agreement amongst ourselves, and he will help us there. Caravaggio is a great artist, but his work divides us. Keep my thoughts to yourself, and make sure Rubens understands that this is only the beginning; nothing has been decided yet."

Baronius knew about the divisions in the College of Cardinals and understood what the Pope was trying to do. He left for Antwerp the next day, but before he went, he sent a message to Fillide asking her to meet him again in the Church of Sant'Anna dei Frenieri. "Nobody must know where this came from," he warned her sternly. "If the story leads back to me, it could place both of us in danger. Caravaggio's enemies, ones who are close to the Pope, are speaking out against his influence. The same with the architect Bernini. I want you to listen and tell me if you hear of any plans to harm Caravaggio. I don't think they'd dare move against Bernini yet. Caravaggio has wealthy patrons who will protect him, and I'll warn them if you hear anything. Remember: you come to me first and only me. No one else. I am trying to do what's best for Rome. That's all you need to know for now."

He realised he was taking a chance in trusting her but could see she had street-smarts and a keen survival instinct. She'd also played a big part in Caravaggio's return, for a fee. She was an operator and would hear if any moves against Caravaggio were planned – before even the

Vatican's spies – so Baronius would hear first, and speed would make him more valuable to the Pope. Fillide was flattered and delighted to be used like this by the Cardinal. She particularly liked the 'for now', which indicated that she was to be a part of any future plans. She would serve him as best she could, and perhaps he could be her entry to the powerful but uneasy world that swirled around the Pope. There would be opportunities, she was sure of that - and confident she could think faster than many men.

Rubens was used to welcoming important visitors to his studio, but he was more anxious than pleased to see Cardinal Baronius. After his return from Naples, he'd tried to put Rome out of his mind, though that was difficult given how much he loved the eternal city. He searched his visitor's face and couldn't see bad news there, but no good news either. "Welcome Cardinal, please rest for a moment. Then, if you wish, I'll show you what we are working on today." "Thank you, maybe later. First, I have an important opportunity for you. The Holy Father asked me to travel and see you personally." Rubens listened in some surprise as Baronius passed on the offer, ending, "Of course this is confidential. Only the three of us know about this." Baronius spelled out in some detail everything the Pope told him, underlining the difficulty of steering plans past Cardinals with conservative views, but also describing the ambitious targets the Pope had for the reformation of Rome. "I understand you will need to think about this. I can stay for as long as you need, then, if you wish, we can travel back for further talks with Pope Urban." The idea of working in Rome again - when the project was Rome itself - was irresistible to Rubens. The Pope was right, there was no commission bigger than this. "If I say yes, what happens to Caravaggio?"

The Cardinal expected this, but the truth was, he didn't know – and, as he explained, neither did anyone else. "He's been pardoned by the Holy Father and can continue to work on anything he chooses. Many wealthy patrons have commissions for him. But nobody can predict what Caravaggio will do next. As for Bernini, he must work with you, or the Pope will appoint another architect. The work will still be done; Rome will be great again." Rubens didn't hesitate. "We travel back to Rome when you have rested. I have to see the Holy Father."

He would talk to the Pope, Caravaggio, and Bernini, and if he thought there was a chance of success, he'd do it. He was sure he could help, but it would be his most difficult assignment yet. "I have a feeling this could be as hard as talking peace with King Philip of Spain and King Charles of England." He paused and reflected, "Harder."

Francesco hadn't given up on the idea of luring Caravaggio back to Malta. He spent some time in Naples admiring the bursts of inspiration that produced Caravaggio's paintings while he was there. Francesco tried to buy his Madonna of the Rosary when he saw the crowds who travelled to see it, but the Colonna family wouldn't sell. "Caravaggio painted this for Naples and the people love it. This is for them," he was told.

"So, the people love it," he said quietly to himself. "That's exactly why I want it for Malta". The painting shows Madonna seated on a throne, holding onto the baby Jesus as a group of the faithful kneel in front of her. It is one of Caravaggio's least controversial works, painted in a period of calm, and a picture that would reflect well on the Knights of Malta. He decided there and then he'd never stop trying to bring Caravaggio to Malta.

When he returned to Rome from Naples, Francesco was tempted to take soldiers with him and confront Fillide Mellandroni over her trickery, but the commander of his personal guard warned him against it. "Choose better ground, my Lord," he said. "In Campo Marzio, we are surrounded by the enemy, civilians and the Capo's men. Not even the Church will save us if we start a riot there. They are wild people; they will attack us and there is no easy escape route."

It was wise counsel, and Francesco remembered the words of Machiavelli: 'Never attempt to win by force what you can win with deception.' He would talk with Mellandroni, use soft words, promise riches and trick her. He knew it wouldn't be easy, she was a formidable woman.

Rubens had a spring in his step when he arrived back in Rome, his favourite place on earth. Before meeting with the Pope, he went to visit Caravaggio, just to see how he'd settled in. He wasn't going to mention the Pope's plan about them working together. That was some way down the road - if it ever happened at all. His first problem was getting in to see him. When he went to Caravaggio's favourite bar he was stopped at the door by two of the Capo's men. Tomassoni was taking no chances; two guards went with Caravaggio every time he went out, and another one stayed close by when he was at home. He'd gradually accepted the situation and either ignored them when he was working or brought them into his company when he went out.

The Capo recruited carefully: the guards had to be flexible and ready to listen. He didn't want Caravaggio getting into a fight with his protectors, which was always possible. "Rubens - Mio Amico!" Caravaggio hailed him and waved his guards away from the door, telling them, "This is one of the finest painters in Europe - not dangerous at all, molto diplomatico." Smiling in welcome, he greeted Rubens. "You have followed me, and you see how safe I am. Buoni Amica protects me all the time. Nothing bad has happened, and I'm working in Bellisima Roma, so nothing can go wrong, can it?"

He gestured to the guards and Rubens joined in the general laughter. "Except when he has too much vino," one of the guards said. "No such thing as too much wine," Caravaggio corrected him. "Especially when Rubens comes all the way from cold, rainy Antwerp." Rubens was relieved to see Caravaggio in such good humour and began to feel more relaxed about his mission. Maybe something could be arranged? He checked himself and remembered the words of Caravaggio's friend Mario Minitti, "He's addicted to danger; he looks for crisis, always." As they talked together into the night, the guards grew bored with a conversation they couldn't join, but they didn't leave Caravaggio and ignored his constant invitations to enjoy a glass of wine. Rubens was impressed: it seemed as if the Capo had injected some discipline into his organisation. Caravaggio was so happy Rubens was tempted to explain why he'd come to Rome, but caution took over. They agreed to meet again soon, and the guards made sure Caravaggio got home safely.

Fillide heard about the visit early the following morning. Sandro had won the confidence of the guards, inventing a story about how he was helping his uncle. He promised them a reward if they brought him news of any visitors or people enquiring about the famous artist. "They told me a famous artist called Rubens came to see Caravaggio, and he was pleased to see him. They talked about painting for hours and how he was working with Bernini on plans for new buildings. Caravaggio got excited and drank too much. Rubens said he'd see him again soon as he's staying in Rome for a while."

"So Caravaggio didn't seem worried?" she asked. "No, they said he was happy - excited, even," Sandro told her. "The guards won't let anyone near him if they think they might upset him. They've been warned there will be consequences for them if anything happens to him. And they're very frightened of the Capo."

On the surface, it didn't seem as if Rubens was any kind of threat. Fillide remembered him from the night Ranuccio was killed, and she knew Caravaggio liked him, but she wasn't going to let what seemed like an innocent meeting pass her by.

She had to know more about Rubens and went to see Onorio, who she guessed would have heard of him. "He's one of the leaders of Renaissance painting," he told her. "Works for the Royal courts of Europe... England, Spain, France, and here in Rome for rich patrons. He's a famous man, gets on well with powerful people." Then a thought came to him; he knew Fillide wasn't asking him some casual question. "Do you think he's here to work with Bernini?"

The idea that Rubens was here to replace Caravaggio, to take his place at the right hand of Bernini had flashed through her mind as soon as Onorio explained how famous Rubens was. "Would Rubens be interested in that?" she asked. "Maybe.

Who wouldn't want the chance to leave their mark on Rome? He's got the talent, and he's better known than Caravaggio. But does Bernini want somebody as famous as Rubens working with him? I don't think so: he'd be worried Rubens would steal some of his glory. Bernini thinks he doesn't need help from anybody because he knows everything already." Onorio spoke bitterly. Had they been in a bar, he'd have spat on the floor at the mention of Bernini.

Fillide didn't react to him, but inside, a bolt hit her. A man like Rubens didn't travel to Rome by chance. This was what Cardinal Baronius had feared. Disruption was on the way, and it was bad news for Caravaggio. She chose her words carefully: "It might not be anything, just two friends meeting. The Capo is protecting Caravaggio every way he can. Don't say anything, for now, I'll see what I can find out."

When she told Cardinal Baronius about the meeting, she got the feeling he wasn't surprised. He simply asked about Caravaggio: if he seemed agitated and if he was pleased to see Rubens. When she said he was happy and friendly he smiled and nodded. "Rubens is someone he respects. He's recommended Caravaggio to patrons in the past. This could be nothing, we'll have to wait and see."

"Is Rubens going to take Caravaggio's place and work with Bernini?" Fillide asked directly. She had to get to the point. "We wait and see," the

Cardinal repeated. "Rubens is a diplomat, a careful man. We must be careful too: you and I may have a part to play in this. Keep a close watch on what happens in Marzio, and tell me straight away if Caravaggio starts to argue and fight with everyone. That will be the sign."

Fillide knew Baronius wasn't telling her the whole story, but it wasn't a problem. She'd heard enough for now and thought to herself, "This affair isn't over, it's only just starting." She hurried back to her apartment where Sandro was waiting with more news. "Francesco is back, and he's asking about you."

"Let him ask away," she sneered. "Make sure we have la Guardia close, but I'm not afraid of him." "Shall I talk to him first? Tell him it was all a misunderstanding?" Sandro suggested. Fillide laughed but agreed, and he came back saying Francesco was all sweet words and calm. "He still wants Caravaggio to work for their Church. But here's the big thing: now he says he'll put five thousand Scudi on the table if we can get Caravaggio to go to Malta. He's desperate, I bet he'd pay twice that."

"Well, the Capo says he stays in Marzio and so do many others," Fillide told him. "People more important than him. If we go against them we're dead. Shame really, five thousand is a good figure," she mused.

Fillide had ambitions that extended beyond Campo Marzio. She wanted to move one day, away from the constant need to hustle for money, certainly before her looks faded. A rich husband would be one solution, money of her own a better one. Then, maybe she could move up the social scale, even buy her own home.

Over the next couple of days, she hugged the thought, dreaming big dreams. Her own palazzo in pink and white marble. There would be a bubbling fountain outside, a grand staircase inside leading to an elegant salon and many bedrooms. With money of her own, she wouldn't have to marry some old man. She could choose anyone she wanted; Sandro would do to start with.

At twenty-five, Sandro was also starting to make plans. So far, he'd accepted that she was the dominant one. Without her he was just the the Capo's nephew. What's more she was smarter than him, he couldn't deny that and she had contacts who were out of his reach. Yet she needed him and together they were stronger - he was sure of that. She might not agree, but at the right moment he'd tell her he was a big part of their success together.

Fillide's Palazzo dreams were interrupted when Onorio came calling with thoughts about his number one preoccupation. He'd never stopped thinking about it, and she could be the key. "Suppose Bernini didn't have Caravaggio working with him and was told to work with Rubens instead

- he might walk away from the whole project, and they'd need a new architect."

"Now, I just wonder who that could be," Fillide mocked him, though it did seem like some jagged shapes were starting to fit together. If Rubens did take over, maybe Caravaggio could be persuaded to go to Malta. It wouldn't have to be forever, and perhaps an arrangement that kept him happy could be worked out. As for Onorio taking over from Bernini, that was a different story. She'd have to slow him down. If he tried to get things started by himself it would be a disaster - a fatal one if the Capo heard they were scheming to move Caravaggio to Malta.

She decided to try and organise a 'casual' meeting with Rubens and find out as much as she could, without revealing how much she already knew. Striving to come up with a plan, she eventually settled on a 'Welcome Home' party for Caravaggio. One late afternoon, she visited his studio together with Sandro and arrived flamboyantly waving a bottle of his favourite wine. Climbing onto a table, she made a mock formal speech. "Michelangelo Merisi," she announced, using his birth name, "Now you're back in Rome, as one of our most famous citizens, pardoned by the Pope and no longer a wanted man - we must celebrate, it's time to throw a party."

She saw the look of amazement on his face and burst out laughing. He made a grab at the bottle, but she pushed him away. "Wait! I'll organise it. Make sure all of your friends are here, but none of your enemies. We don't want any more fights! It will be your special 'Welcome Back Party,' what do you say?"

Caravaggio liked Fillide. They'd spent a lot of time together when he used her as a model, even been lovers briefly. He knew she was unpredictable, and he respected her but he had no idea of the part she'd played in his return. "Yes, yes, give me the bottle now!" He laughed and lifted her down from the table. He'd been back a month, work was going well he was relaxed. He talked with Sandro about their journey from Naples and asked about the soldiers, Petronio and Troppa. "Yes, I heard about them," Fillide said. "Two heroes, they'll be here." Gradually she turned the conversation around to other people to invite. "I hear there's a very important artist friend of yours in Rome."

"Rubens, yes he should come," Caravaggio agreed. "He came to Naples and tried to persuade me not to return, but now I'm here!" Laughing, he looked appraisingly at Fillide. "He might want you to model for him, but now I see you again, maybe not. You're too thin! Rubens likes his models with plenty of flesh on their bones. He loves them like this..." Standing up, he stretched his arms wide and sketched the generous proportions of a Rubens model. "He told me he has a new sixteen-year-old wife, and she is like this," he sketched a pregnant stomach. "He keeps her pregnant all the time! Maybe Sandro should do the same with you!"

Fillide pulled a face in mock horror, "Caravaggio, you know me better than that!" "She's too careful!" Sandro said which was absolutely true. They drank the bottle, bought another one, then left after they'd fixed a date for the party.

Rubens had been thinking for a long time about the opportunity he'd been offered, debating with himself. He didn't dare to talk to anyone. Eventually, he attended an audience with the Pope. "Holy Father, I know this is a delicate matter, but when the project is big, we must expect problems along the road." Since his meeting with Caravaggio, he'd decided it would be too difficult to work in partnership with him. Their talk had been socially friendly and relaxed, but he realised how significantly different their relationship would be in a working situation.

Egos would clash. He was used to working in his own studio with artists who recognised him as their leader. His vision was the one that counted, the others were there to follow.

Caravaggio would never accept a situation like that. Working with Bernini he was an equally valuable partner. They worked in different mediums, but ultimately their vision came together. Rubens couldn't imagine how he fitted into that partnership. His diplomatic skills would have no effect on Caravaggio's dynamic thinking.

"I understand your difficulties," Rubens said and hesitated. Maybe the Pope wanted to lead the conversation, and out of deference he waited, but the Pope's neutral expression didn't change so he continued. "Many of your cardinals see the work of Bernini and Caravaggio as sinful and dangerous. I can't change that. What I could do, possibly, is work with Bernini and create the new Rome we all dream about. A Rome we could all worship together. But I can't do that working with Caravaggio. At first, I thought it might be possible, but when I see him here in Rome, working, I see he is fixed - set on a road with Bernini he will never leave. He is a genius but a singular one."

Pope Urban sighed, "This is where we are. Thank you, Peter Paul, for thinking about our dilemma. I agree, Bernini and Caravaggio are brilliant, adventurous, but if we cannot accept their vision, that's how it will remain: a vision. Not the reborn Rome we want. I am a spiritual leader Rubens - and a practical man. I want to see the new Rome. The people need it. I need it. Most of all, for the counter-reformation, the Church needs it. I will speak with Bernini and ask him to work with you. If he refuses, we start again. Rome is the eternal city, but I don't have an eternity. I am mortal. One way or another, we go forward." Rubens thanked him for the opportunity and said that if that was what he wanted, he was ready to give everything for the Church and Rome. He then asked the question. "Your Holiness, Caravaggio is my friend, and he has many other ways to serve the Church. What happens to him now?"

"That depends on his behaviour. He has to obey the law. Rome is a dangerous place for those who don't." Rubens took that as a direct warning. The Pope's expression gave nothing away, but the meaning was clear. Rome was eternal, patience wasn't. Bernini's conversation with the Pope was tense. He'd heard there were murmurings from important cardinals about his work but had no idea the Pope would take them so seriously. The Pope didn't spare him. He laid out the situation and told him this wasn't a discussion; it was a choice. Accept the terms or go. Shaken, because he thought the Pope was a friend and supporter, he tried to argue but the Pope cut him off. "You have to be mature about this. These are big decisions, and I don't take them without good reason. We go forward with you, or without you. I have to know by the end of the day." Later the Pope told Cardinal Baronius what had happened. "I think Bernini will swallow hard and stay. He's a fool if he doesn't, and we don't need fools. I want you to watch Caravaggio and Campo Marzio carefully. His work is astounding, but private patrons will have to support him; the Church can't any longer. As for Marzio, a place like that must be run properly, with authority, or it drags us all down. See that it is."

Baronius thought the Capo and the courts should be the ones to handle that but didn't say so. Maybe the new Pope wanted the citizens to know who was in charge, even when they were at play. He didn't have a problem with that. It was all part of the bigger picture. More power to him. Bernini accepted the new terms; the opportunity wouldn't come along again in his lifetime. His immediate problem was telling Caravaggio he'd been sidelined. He'd seen the man on the rampage; calm and Caravaggio didn't go together, so he simply spoke about delays in the next commission and talked about a wealthy patron he knew who was eager to give him work. Caravaggio seemed to accept the news. After all, many patrons had spoken to him since his return. But the prospect of a break in his work brought complications. With time on his hands, he began to wander the streets again, meeting with friends in bars and listening to the latest gossip about commissions. When he heard that his great patron Cardinal Borghese had placed an important church commission with one of his rivals, Raphael, his mood darkened. His obsessions turned into loud arguments with innocent victims in the street, and he had to be rescued by the Capo's guards. Even worse, he met Bernini by chance and began a violent argument with him that only ended when the architect turned and ran, fearing for his life. Realising what he had done, Caravaggio apologised the next day, blaming the incident on drink, but began to fear he wouldn't work with Bernini again.

Sandro heard about the argument from Caravaggio's guards, and when he told Fillide, she rushed to tell Baronius. "He's probably heard about a decision the Pope made," he began to explain. First, he made her swear on the Bible she wouldn't repeat what he was about to say. "The Pope called Bernini to the Vatican and told him he had to work with Rubens, not Caravaggio. The College of Cardinals thinks Caravaggio's paintings are blasphemous. When Caravaggio finds out, he's going to be a danger to himself and others. If he does something stupid like last time, it's all over. This new Pope won't help him. Campo Marzio has to be careful too. His Holiness told me he won't stand for further problems - he'll close everything down."

Fillide listened carefully. This could change everything. The last thing she wanted was attacks from above on the Marzio, but maybe she could swing the situation her way. Bearing in mind what Baronius had said about being careful, she thought she'd better warn him about the party for Caravaggio. "Just make sure you make him happy, not angry," was his only comment. By the time Fillide got back to Marzio, she already had the beginnings of a plan. "If Caravaggio has to leave Marzio - and I think he will - we know where he can go. We'll get him to Malta and make five thousand

Scudi," she told Sandro. "Maybe more," Sandro said, "but he doesn't want to go." They both thought for a moment before Sandro continued. "Suppose Caravaggio gets drunk at the party? Or better still, we put something in his wine. Then, when he wakes up, he'll find out he's on the way to Malta."

"You make it sound easy, but you've forgotten about the Capo. What happens when he finds out Caravaggio's gone?" Fillide asked. "He'll blame us, and we'll go to jail, or he'll have us killed."

"That won't happen if Caravaggio does something terrible, and then escapes. It won't be our fault, and this time everyone will say we're better off without him, even the Capo. And anyway, he isn't the only talented painter in the world. More trouble than he's worth, some say."

"So, you're an art expert now?" Fillide asked, not convinced about his plan. "And what is this 'something terrible'?"

"He's liable to stab someone," Sandro said carelessly. "He's started wearing his sword at all times, and you know how easily loses his mind. Let's just hope it isn't you or me." He hugged her protectively. His Tomassoni side was coming out: to him, blood and violence were essential tools. "We have to be in control."

"You're talking about getting someone drunk and arranging for them to stab someone! How can we control that!?" Fillide demanded.

Sandro had an answer to that. "We'll have our own people there. I'll bring them in from Naples - Camorra people. Nobody from around here will know them, and we won't be connected."

"No! Nobody needs to get stabbed," Fillide said angrily, but Sandro retorted. "So how do we explain to the Capo that he's disappeared? What's the story?" Fillide was thinking fast. She knew one way or another there was going to be a crisis. Caravaggio couldn't help himself; he was upset and angry. His whole life had been a drama, and that wasn't going to change, but Sandro was right about one thing: they had to be in control. To just let it happen would be a disaster.

"What if we tell Francesco we know where Caravaggio is, and they can come and get him. When they arrive Caravaggio is drunk, unconscious. Francesco turns up with his men, and they just grab him, put him on a ship and sail off to Malta. That way Caravaggio's gone and it's not our fault. You still bring in the Camorra, because you're right, we do need to stay in control. If anything goes wrong at the party, we have to take charge and make sure Caravaggio stays with us. Then our story to the Capo is how we saved him. We say Francesco came in with his men and tried to kidnap him, but he's still here because we saved him. Francesco will start screaming about how we arranged the whole thing, but it's his word against ours - and the Capo's got to believe his own nephew, right?"

Sandro wasn't sure about that but agreed to go along with her. She usually got her own way, and five thousand was a game-changer. Fillide decided her best weapons in approaching Francesco were lies, flattery and lust. She hadn't cheated him, she'd say, it was simply a misunderstanding about dates. She was deeply sorry, but these things happened. For the meeting, she decided to take over a whole café and lay on a generous lunch for him and his officers. In her message suggesting the meeting, she told him some of the most beautiful courtesans in Marzio would arrive after their business was over. Naturally, they were included in the hospitality, and private rooms were available for entertainment. She concluded, "If all your officers are as handsome as you, I'm sure they'll enjoy the occasion." Francesco smiled when he got her message. "She's silky smooth," he told his senior commander, "but we can't trust her an inch. I won't relax until we have Caravaggio in our hands. Let's enjoy the lunch and whatever happens afterwards. We'll make the arrangements, charter a boat to take us back to Malta, and take as many soldiers as we need to secure Caravaggio. Choose your most disciplined men. We have to be smart; this is dangerous."

The lunch went as well as Fillide hoped. When Francesco arrived, she greeted him like a returning lover as Sandro waited discreetly in the background with four Camorra heavyweights in case negotiations broke down. Wine sweetened with honey was served, and Fillide poured generous measures. "No water on the tables," she told café staff, "I want everyone to enjoy the wine as it comes." As strong as possible was what she meant, not diluted.

As they ate, she told Francesco that Caravaggio was concentrating on work at the moment, but they were throwing a party in his honour, welcoming him back to Rome.

"We'll make it easy for you. The party will be in a bar near the docks, so you'll be able to take him straight to your boat. We have a special drink for him that will make him incredibly happy, and then he'll just fall asleep. We'll carry him out, say we're taking him home and you'll be waiting." Francesco said it sounded like a good plan. He could see it working in a place like Marzio. She waited for the right moment, just before the courtesans were due to arrive, to bring up the question of money. "I know you offered five thousand Scudi when you talked to Sandro, but for the risks we're taking, that's not enough. Remember, the Capo has been instructed to guard him, so our risk is great. We're offering you an easier way to take him. You don't have to do anything. So, ten thousand is what we need, but of course... I might add some extras, especially for you." She slipped a hand onto his thigh, making it clear what the extras would be. Not long afterwards, they agreed on seven thousand. After all, she was the most famous courtesan in Rome, and her favours didn't come cheaply. The deal was seven thousand Scudi to be handed over once he had Caravaggio in his grasp. With that settled, the lunch party moved upstairs to their reserved rooms. Fillide managed a quick wink to Sandro as she passed by. Their future was looking brighter.

When Rubens and Bernini finally met, they found themselves bound together by their faith and beliefs. They were both devout Catholics, and both believed in the supremacy of the Pope. Rubens loved Rome from the day he first arrived there and was as dedicated as Bernini to re-establishing it as the greatest city in the world. He was determined to help in any way he could.

Their collaboration began when Bernini visited Antwerp and saw Rubens' altarpiece for St Paul's Church. The passionate Italian in him saw how their faith stretched beyond national borders and bound them together. Rubens' masterpiece became the inspiration for the Cathedra Petri, the grand finale to his designs at St Peter's.

"This will be one of my greatest works," Bernini told Rubens, "a tribute to the supreme power of the Holy Father." It was a meeting of minds; Rubens knew their partnership was going to work. Bernini told him about his encounter with Caravaggio. "He seemed almost out of his mind. There was no way to tell him his work wasn't over, that he was going to get big commissions from wealthy patrons. He blamed me for everything. He said I must have turned the Pope against him - I thought he was going to kill me!"

Rubens sympathised; he'd seen the way Caravaggio worked himself into a rage. "Did he mention me?" he asked. "No, it's me he blames. I'm just going to stay away, make sure I don't meet him again. He's always been a wild man, but rich patrons don't care; he's that good. The original - a true genius."

"I tried to get him to stay in Naples," Rubens said sadly. "Cardinal Colonna will always protect him."

"Well, he's got the Capo of Campo Marzio protecting him now," Bernini said. "I know," Rubens replied, "that's the problem. He'd be safer jumping into a pit of snakes." He was so worried he decided to make one more effort to get Caravaggio out of Rome and back to Naples.

Philip E. Rowson

The Capo follows his nose

Giovanni Tomassoni was taking his responsibility for Caravaggio's welfare and behaviour seriously. The guards had to report daily on where he'd been and who he'd seen. When the names of Fillide and Sandro cropped up together with details of Caravaggio's welcome home party, his instincts twitched. Why was his nephew involved? He knew Sandro was with Fillide Mellandroni, but why would he be going to what looked like a cultural event? This was for the artistic community, not a man like Sandro. When he was told his nephew had also been seen with Camorra gang members, he had to find out more.

"So, nephew, taking an interest in the arts these days, are you?" he asked sarcastically. Sandro hadn't been pleased to get the message to see his uncle; he suspected it wasn't a casual invitation. "Not really. It's just a party," he replied.

"Tell me, why were you with Marco Esposito and Andrea Ricci two days ago?" Tomassoni demanded, his tone sharper. "We don't want these people visiting Marzio. We have our own thieves.

We don't need to bring people from Naples to come and steal from us." Sandro groaned inside. They'd kept to the shadows when they met, but still, his uncle had eyes everywhere.

"Now, tell me it's nothing to do with Caravaggio. I have people to guard him, keep him away from trouble, but you bring it right to our door. Why?"

"These people are just friends from when I worked in Naples. They were in Rome, so they came to see me. I gave them food before they caught the boat back. That's it, nothing to do with Caravaggio. They've no idea who or what he is. All they really wanted was for me to find some women. They said they'd do the same for me in Naples." That was true enough. After he'd told them about the party and what he wanted, Sandro had taken them to the best brothel in Marzio. As the Capo's nephew, he was royally treated, and the visitors were entertained for free. The following day, they were happy and told Sandro he could rely on them.

The Capo listened sceptically to this story. He knew Sandro was getting ever closer to Fillide and that the relationship was more than professional. But he'd also been told in no uncertain terms that Sandro wasn't in charge. "He's obsessed, does everything she says," said one of Sandro's friends who was keen to stay in favour with the Capo. "I hear Mellandroni's moving up in the world, but I know what she is, even if you don't," Giovanni said scornfully as Sandro winced. "Tell her I'm watching, and I might come to this party. Everything Caravaggio does, I must know. So be careful: if anything happens to Caravaggio, I won't help you."

This was a serious threat, and it made Sandro wary. For the moment he simply warned the Camorra team to stay off the streets. Altogether there were five gang members, and on the night of the party, he was counting on them to stick with him no matter what.

He told Fillide about the meeting with the Capo and added, "We might have to run after this, Giovanni's getting too close."

"If he comes to the party, the whole thing's off," she said immediately. "We'll tell him Francesco's waiting, trying to grab Caravaggio, but we're protecting him. Then it's up to him what he does. We'll be in the clear." She wasn't as relaxed and confident as she sounded. Only the thought of the money kept her going -although they might have to sacrifice it if the Capo did arrive. Which would be a shame, because what she didn't tell Sandro was that she'd seen Francesco again and they'd enjoyed uninhibited sex. Naturally, he had to pay. After an afternoon in her bed, she'd managed to get the fee raised back to the ten thousand she first asked for.

Her unrestrained lovemaking sealed the deal. Fillide aroused him more than any other woman, and her Marzio honed skills kept him in action for longer. Like Sandro, he was besotted with her. He could hardly think of anything else and began to dream of taking her back to Malta. She wondered how they might still get the ten thousand off him - even if he didn't leave with his prized artist. Was that possible?

As for Sandro, a dangerous moment was approaching. He could see Caravaggio was exhausted when he arrived at the party and knew that could lead to the artist's manic mood changes. Insecurity about his work left him in a constant state of anxiety and he'd just finished a commission for Cardinal Borghese.

But there were always moments of exhilaration too. Once again, he'd felt the power flowing through him as he painted in a fury of creativity. The result was The Crowning with Thorns, a picture both horrifying and beautiful. Two soldiers are brutally fixing the crown to the head of Christ, using sticks as levers, enabling them to force the thorns deeper into his scalp. The horror is magnified by the casual indifference of another soldier who simply stands and watches. Christ wears an expression of forgiveness for their vindictiveness. Caravaggio's Chiaroscuro technique captured the emotional charge of the scene. He brought the distant moment of suffering into sharp, present-day focus. The result is a masterpiece of reality painting, revealing again why he was the religious communicator of the age.

Ironically this was the quality Pope Urban VIII wanted for the counter reformation although he knew his Cardinals had set their minds against him. Sandro began to relax slightly as he saw Caravaggio's joy when he recognised the street friends gathered to meet him. It was going to be a loud but happy occasion. He greeted Rubens affectionally and described the painting to him in eloquent detail.

"I can't wait to see it, my friend," Rubens said excitedly, caught up in Caravaggio's enthusiasm. "Cardinal Borghese will be a lucky man to have a painting like this on his walls. It sounds like a genuine Caravaggio! Let's drink to that." Right on cue, Fillide came forward with the wine she'd doctored to taste sweet but also strong enough to bring deep sleep.

"Drink it down my friend, you deserve it," she urged him. To her delight, he took a huge gulp and licked his lips. The party spirit swelled, driven by humour, scandalous stories and the plentiful supply of wine Fillide provided. She kept Caravaggio's special bottle by her side and topped up his glass regularly. Sandro whispered in her ear that Francesco and his men were waiting outside. "Tell them to wait an hour and he'll be asleep," she said.

Caravaggio was enjoying himself and insisted his two guards join in. "Come on, the Capo's at home sleeping," he laughed. "More wine here," he shouted to Fillide. She poured a good measure for him and a couple of generous glasses for his guards. Urged on by Caravaggio, they were soon drinking along. Outside, Francesco and his men waited patiently. He'd brought the money: there was no point trying to cheat Fillide on her home ground and he didn't want to anyway. Sandro came out again and told him everything was going to plan. Or at least it was until he saw the Capo and five of his guards coming their way.

Ducking down, he went back into the party and told Fillide. "Don't tell him about Francesco," he said before she could speak. "I'll handle this." His tone was authoritative, decisive. He showed her his dagger and the breastplate he was wearing under his shirt. Sandro had thought about his position. What would he do if his uncle did come? He could tell him everything and survive. He'd be a marked man - but he'd remain alive. If he didn't tell him, he had no idea what would happen. In that moment, he made his decision. He was the next generation; this was going to be his time. When his uncle found out about the plan, he knew there would be no mercy – and he wasn't going to be the one to fall.

That was why he'd brought the Camorra to Rome and to the party. He'd told them there could be a battle, but if they won well enough, they could have a big future in the Marzio. Judging by their reactions, they were happy about that. His instructions were simple, "Wait for my signal, then strike hard and we'll take them, they're not expecting trouble. We need them dead."

Fillide was also running through her options. The first was to forget what Sandro said and tell the Capo about Francesco as soon as he came through the door. Then she'd have to take a chance on whether he believed her story about protecting Caravaggio. Alternatively, she could keep quiet and see what happened.

In different ways, Sandro, Francesco, and the Capo would have a big part to play in her future.

She looked across at Sandro as he watched the door. There was strength in the way he stood. She'd seen men like that before. Her every instinct told her to have faith in him. She was going to wait and see how this went. The Capo came through the door, scanning the crowded room quickly. Maybe he'd been tipped off, but she couldn't be sure.

"Benvenuto Capo, always a pleasure to see you," Fillide greeted him with just the right amount of deference. He didn't reply. He was looking for Caravaggio and nodded as one of his guards pointed him out. Rubens saw the Capo first and tugged at Caravaggio's sleeve. "We have a visitor." Caravaggio broke off his conversation and scowled when he saw who it was.

"Giovanni Tomassoni, the second most important man in Campo Marzio," he shouted mockingly and awaited a response. The Capo ignored him and jabbed an aggressive finger at the guards sitting alongside Caravaggio. Before they could speak he leaned across the table and shouted in their faces. "What's happening here, why are you half drunk?"

Caravaggio reacted first, stumbling to his feet, fueled by the wine. "Don't worry, they'll be completely drunk very soon," he answered mockingly. "They're with me, and they're welcome. It's you that's not invited."

"I don't need any invitations in Marzio, and I say who is welcome and who is not," Tomassoni shot back. He couldn't afford to be spoken to like that in front of his guards. "Watch your tongue and remember the last time we met, Caravaggio. Your important friends won't help you again if you start causing trouble."

"Capo Mio, relax, we're all friends here," Fillide said trying to distract him. Caravaggio's mood was building as she tried to calm the situation. "Have a glass of wine sir, join us," she continued. He ignored the wine and stepped threateningly towards her. "Ah, Mellandroni," he shouted insultingly. "Where's Sandro tonight? They tell me he enjoys the company of cheap prostitutes."

Caravaggio was fully roused now; he wasn't going to let the Capo get away with that. "Tomassoni what's wrong with you? You have no better manners than your brother. Do you remember what happened to him?" It was a wildly provocative question, and in answer the Capo pushed him away so hard he fell backwards over the table, knocking all the glasses onto the floor. He tried to get up, but the wine had got to him; he only made it to his knees then fell back again.

Rubens jumped up to intervene, he wasn't going to wait for the lightning flash of rage but one of Caravaggio's guards grabbed him and pulled him away from the Capo. Like his brother before him, the Capo recognised Rubens as a man of quality and hesitated. This was no common tavern brawler. He introduced himself formally, "I am Giovanni Tomassoni, Capo of Campo Marzio, who are you?"

"Tonight, he's the most important man in Campo Marzio," Caravaggio answered as he finally climbed to his feet. "This is Peter Paul Rubens, one of the most famous artists in Europe and he's my friend. He's here on the orders of Pope Urban to work with Bernini on the rebuilding of Rome. He's a man of quality, and you, Tomassoni, are not. You're the cheap Capo of a red-light district. You have no place in good company." He shouted all this into the face of the Capo and began to fumble at his belt, searching for a dagger.

Antonio Ferrari, one of the guards, leapt between them to protect the Capo and ended up on the floor, pinning the struggling artist down. Rubens knelt to reason with Caravaggio, but his friend's mind was totally lost in a rush of adrenaline. Ferrari was thrown to one side as Caravaggio burst free and stood up. Dagger in hand, he turned angrily towards the Capo.

The movement was the final act of his violent life. Desperate to redeem himself with the Capo, Ferrari instantly stabbed him in the back. The blade pierced a lung and Caravaggio fell to his knees and toppled over. His life was gurgling away as blood pumped onto the floor and Sandro watched from the crowd, unseen by his uncle.

The vicious attack provoked by the Capo sickened his soul. He felt guilty he hadn't stopped it but now it was about survival: him, or his uncle. He shouted to the Camorra and plunged through the crowd towards Tomassoni was looking at the dying Caravaggio in horror. His whole position was under threat again for no good reason. "Idiota!" he raged at Ferrari, "He was no danger, just a drunken fool!"

Then he caught sight of Sandro racing towards him with the Camorra team around him, all armed with knives.

The Capo and his guards didn't have a chance. Sandro was calm, almost detached. Any hesitation would be deadly. Tomassoni died instantly when his nephew stabbed him. Sandro guessed he'd be wearing a breastplate underneath his fine evening cloak, so he struck high. The blade entered above his cheekbone, and the upward thrust tore into his brain. Ferrari attempted to run, but he was blocked, and Sandro stabbed him under the ribs, throwing the full weight of his body into the blow. He was dying as he fell. Without their leader, the remaining guards were demoralised, unprepared, and lost. The devastation of Sandro's attack froze their minds for a vital split second and the Camorra struck.

The killing was merciless, even by the standards of seventeenth-century Rome. One guard managed to run but was caught before he reached the door and died on the spot. In two minutes of havoc, everything changed, and the floor was heaped with silent bleeding bodies. Panting with exhaustion, the attackers turned to face the rest of the party goers. The Camorra were strangers in the Campo and ready to fight on, but there was no need. The fury of the slaughter had unnerved everyone. The ex-legionnaires, Petronio and Troppa, who'd been invited to the party by Caravaggio stood rigid, shocked at the sudden death of their friend. They waited, unsure about what would happen next. They'd seen plenty of hand-to-hand fighting. This was different - a planned massacre. Sandro put his hand up and called for quiet. He knew he had to reassure the crowd. "Everyone here is safe. What happened was not planned, and nothing would have happened if my uncle hadn't come here determined to cause trouble. He's dead and so are his guards. They deserved to die; a great artist did not."

Fillide was shaken, but not so much that she'd forgotten what the night was meant to be about. Whispering in Sandro's ear, she said, "It's not over. Francesco is outside with ten thousand scudi. Collect your men together and we can take it, but we have to move before he finds out what happened. I'll go and tell him we'll be carrying Caravaggio out because he's completely drunk. We can clean him up, wrap him in a blanket and splash some wine around. They're expecting him to be drunk. I'll tell Francesco we don't hand him over 'til we've got the money. Try and gather more men in case it goes wrong. We have to finish this now."

Her instincts never faltered. But after the rush of the killing frenzy, Sandro had gone into shock. His uncle was dead at his feet, all his guards lay dead or dying. When he didn't move, Fillide had to take charge.

Her first move was to call Petronio and Troppa to her side and gather the Camorra around. With Sandro standing silently beside her, she told them what was happening. "Outside, there's a man with money expecting to take Caravaggio away with him. He's expecting him to be drunk and unconscious, so we need to clean him up, wrap him in a blanket and tell them he's drunk. It's dark outside, we'll get away with it so long as we don't let them get too close. If they find out, we take the money anyway, so be ready for a fight - he has soldiers with him. I'll go out now and talk to him. Move now, get Caravaggio ready."

Giancarlo Aldati was the quickest to react, and he began to prepare Caravaggio's body. He sent Troppa to find clean rags to wash him with and quickly bandaged the still bleeding stab wound in his back. Sandro began to recover once he saw how calm Aldati was. Realising that Fillide was outside, he crossed the room to the door, walking carefully around the still bodies, trying not to look too closely. Peering out, he saw her talking to Francesco in what looked like a relaxed conversation.

It was only when he saw how many soldiers Francesco had that he snapped back to reality. They needed to find more men, and the ex-legionnaires were his best bet. Grabbing hold of Troppa he asked, "Can you find reliable men who'd be up for a fight? We need them - now." Troppa thought quickly and nodded, "Some. They must be paid. I have to tell them there's danger"

"Tell them from me I guarantee they'll be well rewarded. Say I'll come to see every one of them. When you have them, bring them round the back." Troppa nodded and disappeared at speed. He knew he could drag old comrades out of their favourite bar with the promise of a payday.

Fillide was at her most reassuring as she chatted to Francesco. "Caravaggio's in good spirits and drinking well," she assured him. "What he doesn't know is that he's drinking 'sleeping wine' and will be gone soon." Then, looking around, she asked, "You've got the money?" "As soon as we have him, you'll get what we agreed," he replied. "Show me. We don't want any misunderstanding, and we have soldiers with us."

Francesco took her to a small cart guarded by three soldiers. A large chest was standing on it, and Francesco opened the lid to reveal piles of coins. "Put your hand deep down inside to make sure it's all coin. The Knights of Malta aren't thieves or robbers." She did as he said and plunged her hand in, pulling out a handful of florins. "We have a deal," she told him. "And we have an agreement, don't we?" he asked, caressing her round the waist. "Of course. I'll visit you in Malta in the spring - I'm looking forward to it," she told him with a suggestive smile. "We're good together." She squeezed his hand, "Bring the coin closer to the door, and while it's being counted we'll have an hour together before you go. I'll see if he's asleep yet." She went back inside, leaving Francesco aroused but unready, totally off guard.

Fillide seals the deal

Rubens was easily the most grief-stricken man in the room. He knew what had been lost; Caravaggio had years ahead of him. Of course, he'd seen the strife. Both sides of Caravaggio's personality fighting each other, always at war: the wild street character who couldn't be controlled, and the visionary who captured a scene and brought it unforgettably to life. The master of chiaroscuro whose own life was a dramatic mixture of light and shade. Now, through a series of accidental, unintended events, it was over. Or maybe they were intended. Who had manipulated this scene? Watching Fillide Mellandroni as she moved rapidly about the room, whispering here, instructing there, he was sure he knew part of the answer. The first time he'd seen her she was with Caravaggio: drunk, fiery, and beautiful. She'd caused the argument between him and the Capo's brother. Now she was older and mature, dangerously so. Alive to opportunity, he thought, with her model looks intact. He'd seen her go outside and come back more animated than ever. The men who'd killed the Capo and his men were gathered around her as she talked urgently. Caravaggio's body was moved carefully and respectfully. His staring eyes were closed. A man who looked as if he was comfortable handling bodies wrapped him in a blanket, then, for reasons he didn't understand, splashed wine over his face and clothes. "You must be Caravaggio's friend, Rubens," Sandro said as he approached him with a hand outstretched. "What happened tonight brings shame on Rome. My uncle, Giovanni Tomassini is the cause of it all. Caravaggio hated him and his brother. My uncle should never have come. The party was for Caravaggio. I want to apologize for the death of your friend. He was our friend too; we brought him back from Naples."

Rubens looked Sandro straight in the eye. "I visited him in Naples and tried to persuade him not to come back here because I knew this would happen. Cardinal Colonna was ready to protect him in Naples."

"He was desperate to come back, we simply helped him," Sandro replied. "The Pope pardoned him - sent word he'd be protected."

"Yes, protected by Giovanni Tomassoni! You saw how Caravaggio reacted as soon as he saw him, he knew he was in danger." The normally diplomatic Rubens let his feelings show, he was shaken.

"The man who killed him was part of the protection my uncle set up for him," Sandro replied.

"Everything that happened here was my uncle's fault. We're just trying to make sure this doesn't cause any more trouble. That's why we're taking Caravaggio away soon, and you'll be safer if you stay here for now. Will you do that for me?" Rubens recognised this was an order, not a request.

He had no option; Sandro and his men had just killed six people. Fillide finished talking to the Camorra and joined them. Sandro guessed she wanted to speak to Rubens alone and left. "Caravaggio often spoke about you. He admired your work. I'm sorry I didn't stay with him that night when he killed Ranuccio. I might have stopped it happening," she said. "This is a tragedy that will cause trouble everywhere. He had many friends here in Marzio. They won't forget him."

"Many enemies too. He should never have come back," Rubens said tiredly, "but you knew that."

"Naturalmente. This is my base, it's my business to know. I also know that Cardinal Baronius went to Antwerp to persuade you to come here. You're an important man chosen by His Holiness the Pope. Cardinal Baronius requested my help in dealing with Caravaggio. If you need help while you're in Rome, maybe I can help you too." She felt it was wise to point out that she had connections. Rubens ignored that for the moment. "The Capo has been killed. Are you going to tell the city watch?"

"He was the city watch around here, there's no one else. But Cardinal Baronius will hear soon enough, and you can tell him what happened when you see him. Tomassoni came here acting like a fool and caused Caravaggio's death. That's what I'll say anyway, maybe you can do the same. The Cardinal must hear the truth about what happened tonight."

Rubens knew he was talking to a streetwise operator and certainly didn't want to get involved in the power struggle that was about to start. They were interrupted when four men appeared from a back entrance, talking loudly to Troppa. Sandro went across quickly and quietened them down. "Excuse me," Fillide said, "I have to go. You're our guest, I'll ask Sandro to make sure you're escorted home safely as soon as possible." It was important to get him away from the scene; a battle would start the moment Francesco realised he was being cheated.

The four men joined up with the Camorra by the front entrance and stood waiting. They looked a threatening group. "We wait until his body's taken out. When they have him, we take the money," Sandro told them. Watching on from a distance, Rubens knew the night was far from over. Fillide went outside to tell Francesco they were bringing Caravaggio. "He's completely drunk - unconscious," she said. Before he could speak, she carried on, rushing her words. "Listen, you have to take him now. The Capo's on his way and he'll stop you."

Francesco looked confused, but she continued, "You have to be gone before he gets here." Sandro and his troop of men appeared in the doorway and began walking towards the money, but Francesco was getting agitated. "Fillide, tell them to wait. I have to see Caravaggio first."

"He's here, but the Capo's got guards with him and he's on the way," she told him as Aldati and Troppa approached, carrying Caravaggio's body on an improvised stretcher. "You have to go." Francesco wasn't about to be rushed and grabbed her arm. "I said wait!" Bending down to look closely, he suddenly shouted to Sandro, "Stop, he's dead! Sandro cursed and waved his men forward. "Attacco!" he roared as they charged towards Francesco's soldiers with the Camorra in the lead. When he saw the strength of Sandro's troop, Francesco tightened his grip on Fillide and tried to run, pulling her with him as a hostage. She put up a fight, screaming and struggling even when he had a knife to her throat. Francesco's commander tried to organise his men, but he was cut down in the first onslaught. Three soldiers fell to the savage butchery of Sandro's troop before the rest threw up their arms and surrendered, pleading for mercy. Sandro halted the killing then turned to where Aldati and Troppa had Francesco pinned to the ground. They'd hurled themselves at him, and in the struggle, Fillide got away. An enraged, furious Aldati had his knife at Francesco's throat, but Sandro yelled at him to stop. Killing one of the Knights of Malta would be a fatal mistake. "Tie him up, and we'll ship him back to Malta later. Let the rest go, we have enough bodies to bury." They had the money, the Capo was dead, and so were a lot of the witnesses. Caravaggio was dead too, and there would be repercussions.

Fillide needed to work out their own version of what happened, but her priority was to secure the money. She gave Aldati and Troppa a big fee for their night's work and ordered them to guard it. They'd moved to protect her, and she felt she could trust them. The night was over, but the fallout was beginning. She had to talk to Sandro and get to Cardinal Baronius before the sun went down or there would be more violence.

Baronius was interrupted at dawn prayers by his senior priest who told him that Caravaggio was dead, and there had been many killings in Campo Marzio. "The Capo Tomassoni is one of those killed, but all is quiet now."

"That won't last long. Send twenty men from the Papal Guard to patrol the streets. Tell the commander his mission isn't to cause more trouble, his men are only there to show themselves. Tell the Vatican this is a small problem, no need for them to get involved. I'll look into it."

Most of all, Baronius didn't want the Pope to be alarmed, but equally, he didn't want to say anything until he knew exactly what had happened. Twenty minutes later, a messenger arrived at

Fillide's apartment, and she was taken to a private chapel of Sant'Anna dei Frenieri. "It was all Tomassoni's work," she told Baronius. "He came drunk to Caravaggio's party with his guards and insulted him. I tried to talk to him, to stop him. Even his own guards, the ones he sent to be with Caravaggio, told him it was a mistake for him to be there. But Tomassoni wouldn't listen. He started shouting at Caravaggio, telling him he was immorale. An evil criminal who should have been hanged years ago. He said this time his powerful friends couldn't protect him, and he was going to avenge the death of his brother."

"It was madness. Caravaggio knew they were going to kill him, so he pulled his knife and stabbed the Capo. Then one of the Capo's guards stabbed Caravaggio, and suddenly everyone's fighting, killing, blood everywhere. Sandro Tomassoni, the Capo's nephew, the one who brought Caravaggio back, stopped it all. He had friends from Naples with him and they jumped in - stopped the fighting. Caravaggio was dead - maybe that was always going to happen, who knows? Then another fight started outside, nothing to do with the party, and Sandro stopped that too. It's a miracle he was there, or we would have seen more slaughter. It was a terrible night, and Tomassoni started it all."

"So, Caravaggio killed Tomassoni," Baronius said, thinking it could be much worse. It was believable - maybe too believable. He knew she'd only tell him what she thought would be best received. Truth didn't really come into it.

"And the nephew stepped in to stop it?" This was getting complicated. "Fillide, the Pope has asked me to watch over the Marzio." He was speaking urgently, seriously. "I have to know the truth. Swear to me this is what happened."

"Father, on my mother's life, this is true," she lied. "I'm still shaking just talking about it. Tomassoni was completely mad." She didn't know Baronius had been given authority over the Campo, and it gave her an opening she wasn't going to miss. "If you are thinking about a new Capo, then Sandro, who is young but wise and strong, would be a good choice. Not hot-headed like his stupid uncles, and he's respected in the Campo. Especially after this."

Baronius immediately saw how convenient this was for her, but surely she couldn't have arranged it. Nobody would be surprised that Caravaggio had died a violent death, but a dead Capo was going too far. She obviously knew this Sandro. He didn't believe for a moment that he had suddenly appeared together with useful friends. "So, another Tomassoni. You had an arrangement with Ranuccio didn't you? Are you involved with Sandro in the same way?"

"No," she said quickly. "He's different – swympatico. I've known him for some time, we're friends."

"I have work to do because of all this, Fillide," Baronius said, ending the conversation. "We'll talk again. I have to replace Tomassoni and make sure this doesn't bring us problems now, or in the future. The Pope is very sure he will have peace in Marzio, whatever happens. Listen carefully to everyone and tell me what you hear." He paused and put a hand on her shoulder, looking her straight in the eyes to show how important this was. "I'm putting my trust in you Fillide."

He hurried away, turning the situation over in his mind. Tragic though it was, the death of Caravaggio simplified the situation for the Pope and Bernini. The architect wouldn't be looking over his shoulder every day, wondering if an angry Caravaggio was going to attack him. Keeping the Papal Guard in the Campo would calm the area for now, but it wouldn't be popular with the citizens. He had to appoint a new Capo soon. He wondered if Rubens had heard about the death of his friend but when he got back to the Vatican he discovered the news was everywhere.

He wasn't surprised to be told the Pope wanted to see him and said a quick prayer asking for guidance. A tense hour later, he was back in his office with his senior priest, Father Bianchi. "I managed to convince His Holiness this was all a disastrous, drunken affair and it's under control," he said. "But other voices will whisper in is ear, we have to move fast."

"Maybe the Flemish artist knows something," Bianchi suggested. "I know he was with Caravaggio sometime last week so we should speak to him. There'll will be plenty of gossip and scandal but we need better information than the drunks and thieves of the Campo can supply."

Rubens wasn't surprised to hear from Cardinal Baronius. He'd been dreading the moment. Whatever he said would create problems, so he decided to stick to the facts with no diplomatic cover-ups. Baronius didn't know Rubens was an eye witness and he listened in dismay when he heard his account.

Rome was a violent city but he didn't want Rubens who travelled through the courts of Europe to spread stories of barbarism. "Let's keep this story to ourselves," he suggested. "The holy Father fights every day to protect the name of the Church." Rubens was happy to agree, he was always ready to defend Rome. But what shocked Baronius most was the audacity of Fillide's version. She'd always lived by her survival instincts, but this was another level. She'd moved into a power game worthy of the Senate, not a red-light district, and taken it in her stride. Reflecting later he marvelled at her ingenuity and ruthlessness.

"So, this young man Sandro struck the blow that killed his uncle?" Baronius asked, and Rubens nodded. "And this was after the Capo's guard had killed Caravaggio," he continued, desperate to get the full picture. "Then Sandro and his group killed all the guards who'd arrived with Tomassoni: is that what happened?"

Recalling the scene, Rubens nodded. "It was savage, a battlefield, but Sandro was controlling it from the second he killed his uncle. He didn't hesitate and neither did the others. I can't say it was planned but as soon as Tomassoni entered everything changed. Caravaggio was incensed. He was sure this was going to be just like it was with Ranuccio and he was ready. His reason had gone." Rubens spread his arms, "I'm sorry but nobody could stop it."

"Where was Fillide while this was happening?" Barononius asked.

"She was in the middle of it all. She tried to calm the Capo down as soon as he arrived, but he insulted her, which made Caravaggio worse. He started to threaten Tomassoni. The guard stabbed him to protect the Capo, then Sandro stabbed his uncle. It was a drunken fight that went from bad to disaster in seconds. But there was there was more to it than insults, I'm certain of that and tI have to say, Caravaggio was the most drunk."

"Did you speak with Sandro afterwards?" Baronius asked.

"Yes, he introduced himself and apologised for the death of my friend. He said it brought shame on Rome, but that it was all his uncle's fault,"

Rubens answered. "He was in shock, I think, but controlled. Impressive, considering what happened. Mellandroni was calm. She went around the room, reassuring people. Everyone felt threatened; Sandro's men still had knives in their hands and there were bodies everywhere."

"If you want my opinion, I don't think she was surprised by what happened. Maybe she put Sandro up to it, I'm not sure. He looked to me like a young man who'd grown up fast - a leader."

"My dear Rubens, in all seriousness, I must ask for your discretion," Baronius said. "This just became more complicated. Earlier I spoke to Mellandroni, and her account differs from yours. She said Caravaggio killed Tomassoni, then a guard killed him. When she gave me her version, I thought, 'this story serves you well.' Tomassoni, who was no friend of hers, is dead and now there is a vacancy: we need a new Capo. She has a young, powerful ally who will tell the same story because he's guilty of the murder of an important official. And she has already suggested to me that he would be a good choice for the new Capo. He would be King, and she would be Queen - probably in charge."

Baronius shook his head and waited for a reaction. The drama of this revelation, in addition to what he had personally witnessed, hit Rubens hard. This was Rome, ruthless Rome, but now he was more than a witness; he was part of the story, inside the action. What he said, or reported, would affect everything. He said nothing at that moment but thought intensely, running through the consequences.

"Of course, we can control what other witnesses say," Baronius carried on as Rubens stayed silent, "but there will be many rumours, none of them good. Malicious minds get to work, constructing the story that suits them best. Yet here's the thing: a man of your standing in Rome - and throughout Europe - will be believed. His words accepted."

Rubens still didn't speak, so Baronius continued, "As we know this goes beyond a murderous night in Marzio - we've had many of those before. Together with Bernini, you are responsible for the rebirth of a glorious Rome. That's the Pope's vision. He's built up his coffers. He dreams of this and so do many others. You must not be caught up in this affair which has already cost us one genius who can't be replaced. If your name is dragged into this, you may have to be replaced, and the backward thinkers in the College of Cardinals will have won."

"What do you want of me?" Rubens finally asked. "In many delicate missions I am asked about truth, and I say that in diplomacy there are two kinds: convenient and inconvenient. If we're talking about cause and effect an inconvenient truth causes more harm than a lie. But a convenient truth is much better than either."

Baronius could have cheered. "We understand each other my friend. When the time is right I will inform the Pope. He is fortunate to have found you."

"All armed prophets have been victorious; all unarmed prophets have been destroyed"
Niccolò Machiavelli

The aftermath of the night left Sandro elated, stunned, and worried. When the Papal Guards arrived in the Campo he thought about quickly collecting Fillide and escaping to the country. It wasn't necessary, the Guards did no more than patrol the streets and set up an observation post in the central square. His priority was to pay everyone who'd fought alongside him, so he called a meeting of all who'd been involved, including the Camorra, and put the cash in their hands. He instructed Aldati and Troppa to recruit another five men and told everyone to be ready. "We're not looking for trouble, but it may come our way, so we stick together."

So far, he'd heard nothing from his family, but neither Giovanni nor Ranuccio had been popular, and having a squad around him meant his enemies would think twice. Stories about the way they'd eliminated the Capo and his guards helped, too.

As Machiavelli said, "It's better to be feared than loved if you can't be both." Then there was the pile of money they'd collected. He needed a conversation with Fillide about that. He was ready to split it down the middle, though he wasn't expecting it to be that simple. They had to work together; she'd have to learn to listen to him more often.

The big news came when she got back from meeting with Baronius. "I told him what happened but changed things around a little. I said Caravaggio killed your uncle. I said the Capo arrived drunk and provoked him. Then a guard killed Caravaggio as revenge, and it was all just one big battle which you and some friends stopped from getting worse."

Sandro shook his head. "There will be others who tell him differently, something closer to the truth. But it's done now, we have to think about how we survive."

"We might do better than just survive Amore Mio," she replied. "I told him you were the respected man in Marzio now – that you stepped in and saved the situation. I told him you can do more. He's looking for a new Capo, and I told him you're the one."

Sandro smiled and shook his head; that thought hadn't occurred to him. "No, I can't see that. I think he may have had enough of the Tomassoni family and their problems. Ranuccio is killed, and the Pope himself has to get involved. Now it's Giovanni, and Rome loses a famous artist. Why me?"

Fillide smiled knowingly. "I didn't know this before, but the Pope has ordered Cardinal Baronius to keep a close watch on Marzio. He told him every city has a Marzio: a place where men can go to indulge themselves without upsetting ordinary citizens. It's useful, but it has to be controlled, kept quiet, so the College of Cardinals can pretend it doesn't happen - pretend we're all going to church every day. That's what Marzio is for. The Pope says this, and he's right. Baronius has to keep it that way or he may lose his Cardinal's hat."

"So, he needs a new Capo who can keep order. And here's the best part: he listens to what I say!" she finished gleefully.

"So what happens when he finds out I killed Giovanni, and the rest of us killed his guards? How is that keeping it quiet?" The only thing keeping Sandro from telling her the idea was ridiculous was her history of being right. "Will he listen to you when he finds out you're spinning all kinds of lies?"

"Yes, he will, because he's a practical man and he needs a quick answer," she said firmly. "And why should it matter who killed Giovanni? He's dead, that's what matters. Caravaggio? He's dead too, and that's bad, but it happened."

Fillide had answered him, and now she challenged him. "You stepped up last night and killed your uncle because what he was doing was wrong. Now you can step up and do the right thing again: keep Marzio safe and quiet. Be sure there are big rewards. Giovanni was making a lot of money and so can you."

Sandro wasn't convinced. "It sounds good. You always tell a good story, but I can't believe it's that easy. Baronius doesn't know me! Maybe he thinks I'm just like my uncle. Why should he trust another Tomassoni, and why should he believe you? You're not unknown to the courts, are you?"

"Things are going to change, Sandro." Fillide had a feeling she could talk him into seeing things her way. They'd come this far, now they had to move on. "Remember, a new Pope makes changes because he wants his name to live forever. Urban is doing that. He wants to build a new Rome. So maybe we don't just keep Marzio quiet; we do more. Maybe we can make life a little better for everyone – together. This is our place; we know it better than anyone. Sure, we make money, but we spend it too, making things better. The poor deserve to be helped."

"Caravaggio, God bless his soul, used to say that. It could be his memorial."

Sandro looked at her afresh. He hadn't seen this side of her before, but he believed it. She always shouted and argued when she saw something she thought unjust. He'd put it down to her natural aggression and refusal to be dominated. "So, Citizen of Rome, what do we do next?" he asked mockingly. "Do we have a plan?"

"With me, there's always a plan. You should know that by now, Sandro Tomassoni," she said, rebuking him with a smile. "Number one: remember we have money, ten thousand scudi. We can do a lot with that. But, as I've said from the beginning, the wisest plan is to let me think about money. We decide together, but when you are Capo you will have many things to worry about." She saw his frown deepen and spoke quickly to reassure him. "I only said think about money. We share the ten thousand, half and half; that's only fair, but I think I would be best at managing it. I have more experience with money, using it well. Don't worry, we will always make decisions together. We're partners Sandro."

Reaching out, she hugged him, rested her face on his shoulder, and to her relief, he wrapped his arms around her. "Partners," he said. "Now, we go to bed." He picked her up and carried her over to their letto innamorati.

Father Bianchi knew more about Marzio than his master. He wasn't afraid to visit the bars, cafés and, on occasion, brothels too. So, when he was ordered to go and listen to the gossip, he went willingly. The talk was all about the killing of

Tomassoni and the murder of his guards. Nobody had seen this coming; the Capo and his guards looked like they were in control. The general opinion was that Fillide Mellandroni was behind it all. She was the clever one, with Sandro doing whatever she said.

There was plenty of admiration for what looked like a successful power grab and definitely no grieving for the Capo. "Greedy and stupid," a market trader openly declared to him, pleased he was gone. "Always there with a hand out for money, but never there when you needed him," a brothel keeper said. The death of Caravaggio wasn't such a surprise. His temper and taste for violence was well known.

Bianchi did pick up on one intriguing story. He heard there'd been an even bigger battle outside the party. He was told that Caravaggio's body was being carried out from the party when a huge fight broke out. Soldiers from the Knights of Malta were waiting for Sandro. "But his men slaughtered them," Bianchi was told. "He had some ex-legionnaires from Marzio, but he brought Camorra from Naples, dangerous bastards, they killed plenty." Yet the people who told him this story with some relish didn't know the cause of the dispute. It wasn't until he met Onorio Longhi that he discovered the truth.

Bianchi respected Onorio's father, Martino the Elder, but he knew Onorio was a different personality. He got him drunk and encouraged him to talk about the murder of Tomassoni. "I rejoiced when I heard they killed him, but it's a tragedy Caravaggio's gone. He was my friend, I brought him back from Naples. I see now that I shouldn't have. Rome was too dangerous for him, but he was desperate to come. Tomassoni made me do it."

"Mellandroni is the one who profits from all this," Onorio continued. "They stole a fortune off the Maltese who thought they were going to take Caravaggio back to Malta to paint for them. But Caravaggio was already dead, so Sandro and his Camorra had to kill them to take the money. Mellandroni set it up. She opened her legs for a man called Paulo Francesco - he's one of the Knights of Malta. She tricked him, but they never forget. They'll be back."

Onorio then began to plead with him, "I was promised work on the re-building of Rome - big commissions! Tomassoni said I would get them if I brought Caravaggio back. Now all the work is promised to Bernini, and I get nothing. Talk to the Cardinals; you know what fine work my father did, I can do even better."

Thinking he might be a useful source of information in the future, Bianchi agreed to do what he could. "I know there's money available for the rebuilding, so maybe." Baronius congratulated him when Bianchi delivered his report. "This makes everything clearer," he said. "I have to meet this

Sandro, he sounds interesting. Fix a meeting, outside the city walls, we have to be careful."

After her visit to Baronius, Fillide allowed her mind to indulge in happy thoughts. She and Sandro had come out of the killings unscathed, and her plans had taken on a new dimension ever since she proposed Sandro as the new Capo. Even if that came to nothing, she now had hard cash to support her dreams. Her thinking had long outgrown her apartment. She wanted a Palazzo: one that was grand by the standards of Marzio, and definitely to her own tastes (she wouldn't bother Sandro with the details). What she needed was an architect; someone who could bring the stone and marble of her thoughts to reality.

"Onorio, I'm sorry it didn't work out for you, but at least you got Tomassoni off your back," Fillide said to him as they sat in her apartment. She'd invited him and, full of curiosity, he'd accepted. "Yes, but it cost me my friend Caravaggio," he replied. "Still, if rumours are true, you and Sandro came out on top."

"We had no choice Onorio," she said immediately. She wasn't going to justify herself. "We have to look forward now, and I have work for you. This time, I will pay you." Fillide told him about her plans for a house that would match her new standing. "It's your chance to show what you can do, and it will lead to bigger commissions. You can be the man to bring a new look to Campo Marzio.

There are other people with money here; mine will be the first of many, you'll see."

Onorio bitterly remembered Bernini's taunting him about building new brothels. It was coming true, but she could be right This might be the best offer he'd get for a while. Besides, listening to her talk he knew exactly what she wanted. He could do it, and he promised himself it would look spectacular.

Baronius decided to take Bianchi with him when he met Sandro. Bianchi certainly knew more about Marzio than he did, and Baronius valued his judgement. He'd met Fillide's mother years earlier: she'd been introduced to him at a church gathering and they'd carried on their affair discreetly - he hadn't been sneaking around red-light districts.

"I've heard about the killings and your part in them," he began, sitting opposite Sandro. "I've listened to Fillide and other people who were at the party. My priest, Father Bianchi here, has visited Marzio to hear what people are saying. But I'm not here as a judge, Giovanni Tomassoni is dead, and we need a new Capo. The Holy Father has given me the responsibility of keeping peace in Marzio, and your name has been suggested to me. So, tell me Sandro: can you keep order, make citizens feel safe in their daily life?"

"I hope so. I watched my uncle, and I know I can do better. He wasn't fair or just. People were afraid, so they paid him. I'm different. My name is Tomassoni, but I am not Giovanni or Ranuccio." Baronius studied Sandro as he spoke. Physically, he was powerful, with wide, thick forearms and big hands. Built for handling weapons he thought. The voice was low, the words carefully chosen. "I'll hire good people and pay them properly. That way, we can keep the peace, fairly - without fear," Sandro continued.

"Yet two nights ago, many died," Baronius charged him. "Why should I believe you?"

"They deserved to die - all except Caravaggio. Giovanni was drunk and insulting, and it would have got worse. That's why he had to be stopped," Sandro answered. "I can't make you believe me now, but if you give me the chance, you won't regret it." Sandro's strong presence was reassuring, and Baronius understood why Fillide was obviously close to him. In her life, she needed a Sandro. He'd met the Tomassoni brothers and couldn't imagine them speaking in the same measured way. The young, confident man in front of him was impressive, and time was short. Turning away from Sandro, he whispered in Bianchi's ear. "I'm inclined to say yes. You?"

Bianchi nodded, and the Cardinal turned back to Sandro. "I believe you fell from the other side of the Tomassoni tree," he said. "I'm going to give you this chance. First, I have to speak with the Holy Father, but I'm sure he'll take my recommendation. I'm expecting much of you and I'll be watching, every day. Be true to yourself and don't let me down. Listen to Fillide: she has wisdom: but know she doesn't always speak the truth. Make your own decisions," he said, standing up to leave, "and tell her, the next time I see her, I will ask why she lied me."

The last was said to tell Sandro he knew the truth about the killing of the Capo. As they made their way back to the Vatican, Bianchi hoped he'd done the right thing in 'forgetting' to tell Baronius about the Maltese soldiers Sandro and his men had killed - or the way the Knights of Malta had been deceived and robbed. The Campo needed a strong man in charge, and Sandro had shown ruthless leadership. Sometimes it was best not to know the whole story, he thought to himself, crossing his fingers behind his back.

Philip E. Rowson

"I will build you the first Palazzo of Marzio"

So said Onorio Longhi when he agreed to build a home for Fillide and the new Capo. The budget wasn't as big as he'd hoped, but he was determined to show Roman society what he could do. It was to be a showcase for his style. Set amongst the rundown apartments of the Campo, it would be different; proud and elegant, "Just like you, Fillide," he flattered. "I'll be the judge of that," was the instant retort. He knew she was looking for status - a building to reward her struggles. What he gave her was a three-storey Palazzo with piano nobile, a noble floor with three rooms where she could entertain and impress. The rooms were above street level, away from the crowds and richly decorated with ruby coloured tapestries. High ceilings and fluted columns added a classical feel, with banqueting couches and expensive rugs scattered around."High-class brothel" one guest muttered behind Fillide's back. Onorio didn't object to comments like this (they were half-true). He'd built a home that announced Fillide's position as the powerful partner of the Capo. His design was widely admired for its creative style and won him a series of expensive commissions.

He'd succeeded by breaking simple geometric rules, creating his own form of Baroque architecture just as he'd planned when he first talked to Giovanni Tomassoni. He'd got there by a different route, but his star was rising. Sandro operated on the ground floor, and when he talked to Onorio he said he wanted citizens to know immediately this was a new regime.

Respect would be given - and expected in return. So Onorio had given Palazzo Tomassoni, that was the name insisted on by Sandro, a reassuring, solid feeling. The exterior walls were built with rusticated stone to echo the Roman countryside and decorated with blue marble. There was a balcony over the entrance so Fillide could keep a watch on comings and goings. Both of them were pleased with their new home, and Sandro worked hard to improve conditions in the Marzio.

He survived attacks from his two remaining Tomassoni uncles who were bitterly envious of his success. His bodyguard fought them off and they disappeared. Sandro sent word that next time, they'd be killed. On the rough streets of Marzio, he found he could make good money by offering protection to visitors and traders alike. Fillide used part of their income to invest in a food trading business and a share of the profits from which was used to provide food and lodging for poor families.

It was while carrying out this charitable work that Fillide had a business idea: one that was to last through the centuries.

She realised there was a problem of trust in many transactions. For example: when a market trader was approached by a farmer offering to supply vegetables, to begin with, the goods were fresh, and the price was right. Down the line, though, the trader might demand lower prices, or the farmer might try to supply vegetables that weren't so fresh. Alternatively, the marketman wouldn't pay on time - or pay the agreed price. There was suspicion - a lack of trust that halted the trade and created a blockage.

What was needed, was a third party to settle disputes. If both sides paid a regular fee, the middleman would step in and settle the matter. For example, if the market trader refused to pay on time, he would be threatened, or perhaps his premises damaged. A baker who supplied mouldy bread might be beaten up and have his bakery wrecked. In one way or another, he would suffer. Both sides would soon learn that it paid to trade fairly. The middleman would receive regular fees for keeping trade flowing. Instead of a blockage, there would be three profitable trades.

But the system would only work if the middleman was both respected and ruthless. The retribution suffered by anyone who failed on either end of the deal had to be quick, effective - and feared.

"You and your men have to be that third party," Fillide said, describing the scheme to Sandro. "You keep trade flowing, with profit on both sides, and in return, they pay you regular fees. Soon they'll be coming to you, begging to pay you. You'll be dealing with everyone, getting paid by everyone who wants to trade in Marzio - and many do. We know that."

Sandro listened and thought there was a chance it could work. But he also realised this was a leap into a different world and wondered if he really wanted that. "We're doing okay right now," he said. "Why do we want to get involved with all these people: butchers, bakers, shop keepers – they can all cause trouble."

Fillide half expected this: Sandro wasn't really the one to go looking for extra work. "Look, you don't have to do it all by yourself. You already know how to keep order. You instruct people, and if they don't listen, your men go round and rough them up. Then they do listen. This is the same, only we make more money and get to see how things work in Rome. We don't have to worry about the big families, the cardinals, the courts. We're on the inside."

"Ha! Now you're in fantasy land," Sandro said, determined to bring her back to reality. "We sit here in the Red-Light district with everyone watching us. Not so long ago we killed my uncle the Capo, and his guards. Rome's most famous artist was killed because of us. We robbed the Knights of Malta, and we killed their soldiers. Do we sound like ordinary, law-abiding people with nothing to worry about?"

Fillide had her answer ready. "Do you think all those people, the biggest families in Rome, are law abiding when it doesn't suit them? No. They do what they have to and get away with it, just like we did. And you've forgotten something. Marzio is calm now. Nobody's getting killed anymore, citizens are safe on the streets, all because of you and your men. That's the story. We're just going to make Marzio bigger and better. Remember, this is Rome. Since when did being ordinary and law-abiding get you anywhere?"

Fillide finished triumphantly and laughed. So did Sandro. "Right, il condottiero," he said. "We conquer everyone! You sound like Cesare Borgia!" And act more like Lucrezia Borgia, she thought but kept this from Sandro. She didn't want to worry him. Fillide got her way eventually and persuaded Sandro where their future lay.

They started small. Fillide talked to the tradespeople she knew and explained that Sandro and his men would look after them in disputes - for a small fee, of course. The word soon spread, especially after Giancarlo Aldati and a couple of others wrecked the bar of a man who was slow to pay his bills. He soon paid up, and gradually trade in Marzio was dominated by the new Capo. Fillide was proven right: traders began to approach Sandro and ask to be included in their scheme. He even got requests from other parts of the city - and that was when Fillide got a message to see Baronius.

"You're causing problems for Capos in other parts of Rome," he said, "and they'll complain to the Pope. Sandro is doing a good job. Marzio is calm again. But this protection scheme is too much. Other Capos aren't as well organised as Sandro - they can't do the same and it makes them look bad. They'd like extra money - who wouldn't? But it means more work, maybe danger, so they want it stopped. And they fear Sandro is planning to take over."

Fillide tried to argue that the scheme was good for everyone because trade increased. "Everyone knows where they stand. If a farmer supplies rotten fruit, he's in trouble so he doesn't try it. Same with the butcher, the baker. Tenants pay their rent on time, or try to. We help everyone."

"No, Fillide. You end it. I know it's your idea, Sandro wouldn't think of this. Just remember you are in Marzio, where the brothels and the bars do their trade, where most of the thieves of the city live. You don't get to decide how the rest of Rome runs its affairs. Especially the parts with many fine villas and rich Capos who speak to the Pope, that can't happen."

Baronius wasn't ready to argue, even when Fillide offered to share the fees with them. "No, be content with what you have," he ordered. "Both of you should have been hanged for what you did. If you carry on like this, important people will start to ask questions about what really happened that night and I won't be able to help you. Do you understand?" Fillide nodded. She was disappointed but recognised she wasn't going to win. "Yes Cardinal, I understand. We are grateful for what you did for us, thank you."

She gave him her brightest smile, but inside she was already thinking about how she could get round this setback. Unfortunately for her, Baronius had more. "There's another problem: the Knights of Malta are angry about all kinds of things, some of which are nothing to do with you - but one thing is. Paulo Francisco has requested an audience with His Holiness the Pope, and I know what he plans to say: that he was cheated and robbed by you and Sandro."

Baronius had quickly discovered the full story of their night of killings, but he'd already given Sandro the nod so he said nothing. Then, shortly afterwards, he'd been given more responsibility.

Pope Urban recognised his political skills and he was tired of being constantly asked for favours. He asked Baronius to step in. "Cardinal, I have seen how discreetly you work. A word here, a word there, and meetings with the College of Cardinals nearly always go your way. You know your business well. I want you to control who receives an audience with me. They must speak to you first, and you decide if I should see them. If you're unsure, just ask me, but I have faith in your judgement. Remember, you'll be serving your Pope in an important role."

The move gave Baronius more work but also more power. As the doorkeeper, he had many decisions to make. He could help shape the Pope's policies.

Francisco, the disappointed Knight of Malta, wasn't happy that he had to negotiate this hurdle but there was no alternative. So he told his story with many blood-soaked additions and complaints about Marzio. It wasn't a good idea. Baronius took an instant dislike to him, especially when he insulted Fillide in lurid detail.

He asked her for her side of the story and wasn't surprised to hear a different tale. "He's a born liar, the kind who gives the Church a bad name. He's no celibate priest - not when he's away from Malta. He was planning to kidnap Caravaggio and drag him to Malta to make himself some money. We stopped him and tried to save Caravaggio," Fillide answered instantly. "You can't trust him, he'll say anything."

"I don't trust him. There are many arguments between Rome and the Knights of Malta: about Church land, power, money - the usual. They act like pirates in the seas around Malta. The trouble is it may suit the Pope to listen to him. If he arrests you and Sandro, then he can expect something in return. Perhaps money from the piracy, who knows? That's the way the world works, as you well know. So, tell me Fillide, what do I say to the Pope that will persuade him not to listen to Francisco?"

"Perhaps I could persuade him not to bother His Holiness," Fillide suggested. "He knows he's wrong, and Rome will not give in to him. There are many ways to make this problem go away."

Baronius was sceptical. "He's angry; his dignity's been upset. It will take more than a few nights in your bed Fillide."

"Of course, I know that your Emininence," she replied respectfully. "But he's stupid and always acts according to what happens between his legs. After that, nothing happens between his ears," Fillide was at her most scornful, angry at the thought that a man like Francisco could upset her plans.

"I thought you might say something like that," Baronius couldn't help laughing at Fillide's contempt for a man who considered himself important. "I'm not going to let him get anywhere near the Pope yet, but I won't be able to stall him forever. See what you can do, but don't have him killed. Nothing could save you if that happened."

"We'll give him a night to remember"

Fillide was surprised by Sandro's reaction when she told him about the problems their scheme was causing for Baronius. "So, the rich Capos of Rome don't like us making money here in Marzio? I say we carry on. Let them whine, these sad people!" Fillide agreed with his attitude but knew it wasn't practical and didn't want to let Baronius down after everything he'd done for them.

"Well, maybe we carry on, quietly." Sandro pulled a face, surprised at her restraint but listened when she said she'd come up with a better idea. "Remember that big scandal when Cesare Borgia invited fifty courtesans to his chambers in the Vatican?" she said. "They called it the Night of the Chestnuts. After dinner, all the women danced for the guests, with clothes on at first. Then they moved around the tables and let the guests strip them. They danced a little more, naked, and Cesare Borgia sprinkles chestnuts on the floor. These are for the courtesans, so they go down on their hands and knees, moving amongst them, picking them up to eat. Can you guess what happens next Sandro?" she asked.

"Everybody claps and they're in a perfect position for. . ."

"Yes," Fillide interrupted. "The guests join in, doing what they always do with courtesans, and the Borgias give out prizes to the guests who perform the best."

"I'd have won a prize," Sandro boasted. "Yes, Amore Mio, of course you would. But in our Night to Remember, you don't join in. We put on a special banquet for Francesco, but not in Marzio - he's too scared to come here. We hire a beautiful Palazzo in the city. We'll have to spend some of the money we've made, but we must do it properly. We prepare a feast, bring in the candelabra. There'll be wine and music. So, Francesco performs - badly, of course. He's a terrible lover - but he tries. He tries so hard, that he becomes exhausted and falls ill. Such a shame, and what a scandal for a celibate Knight of Malta to be taking part in a night like that. Then all we have to do is make sure Baronius gets to know about him and what he's like."

They talked more about the idea and how they'd have to hide their part in it. "We need someone with rich friends who'd be ready for an orgy. Shouldn't be too hard to find men like that,"

Fillide said. "But no one from Marzio who can lead people straight to us."

"I know," said Sandro. "What about the Camorra again? But new faces, not the boys already here, they're getting too well known."

Fillide agreed, with conditions. "They must be smart enough to find the right people - bella figura. This isn't some drunken night in Marzio we're setting up: it's an occasion. Francesco has to feel good about it, or he'll get suspicious and run. Last time he was in Rome he nearly got killed. At least this time he gets some excitement."

"It's a shame I won't be there," Sandro said. "I like the sound of this night, it's getting me excited. Come here!" He grabbed Fillide and told her to show him how the women would go on hands and knees, looking for the chestnuts. She got on her knees, offering herself to him. "Like this Sandro. Now show me what you can do."

Paolo Francesco was forced to spend time in penance when the Knights of Malta discovered that his trip to Rome had gone disastrously wrong. But now he wanted revenge. His superiors had agreed to his original plan to bring Caravaggio back to Malta. They enjoyed the prestige his work brought to their churches, and the offerings of pilgrims were even more welcome. They weren't too concerned how he brought Caravaggio back, content to leave the details to him, and although the money was a sizeable loss, they could recoup it. The Knights regularly attacked shipping off their coast, claiming they were defending Christianity against the Muslim forces from North Africa and beyond. In reality, they attacked any vessel that looked likely to be carrying valuable cargo. Even so, they didn't enjoy being tricked by Rome and were ready to listen when Francesco pleaded for another chance. "I want to see this new Pope, ask for justice, and get our money back from these thieves," he told a meeting in Malta's capital, Valetta. They listened and agreed to him travelling to Rome. "Maybe we can make a fresh start with Pope Urban. Tell him how we've been wronged," one church leader said. None of them knew about the meetings with Fillide that had got him into trouble, so they wished him well.

He set off with two soldiers for Rome, and soon he was touring the bars and cafés of the city. Fillide's judgement of his character was sound. The long days in Malta when he was forced to live a celibate life meant that when he had the opportunity, his priority was to hunt for women and sex. When he finally got round to seeing Cardinal Baronius, he was disappointed to discover he wouldn't get an instant audience with the Pope. Previously, the status of the Knights had given him easy access. No longer it seemed and he could tell Baronius wasn't going to support him.

"This tragic night has become a confused and bloody story," the Cardinal told him. "It brought the death of one of the most respected and talented artists in Italy, one who Pope Urban VIII was going to reward with important commissions. His work was important to the Holy Catholic Church."

Francesco protested that Caravaggio's death had nothing to do with him. "It was the work of that filthy whore Mellandroni and the people who robbed me."

"A Capo appointed by the Pope was also killed," Baronius continued. "The Holy Father may not wish to see anyone associated with this terrible night. He has many calls on his time, his mission to support the renaissance cannot stop, and nobody is sure of the facts. But because we respect the Knights of Malta, I'll see what can be done."

So, Francesco had to wait, and news soon reached Fillide that he was touring the bars and brothels of Rome but staying away from Marzio. "We have this plump bird fattening himself with tasty treats every night," she told Sandro. "I'll start preparing the big night - his final plucking." She'd decided that Onorio Longhi would be perfect as a frontman to host the night. He was well known among the city's nightlife as a partygoer - a man with rich friends and clients. "I'll tell him it's a thank-you party. For him and someone else who's been helping us," she told Sandro. "I'll say we want it to be a big surprise, and that's why we won't be there to start with."

"Do you think he can handle it?" Sandro asked. "He's got a big mouth; we don't need him to spread the story all over Rome." Fillide agreed he had a point but still thought he was the right man.

"Maybe if you're there when I tell him, that will convince him we're serious. He's frightened of you."

"I'm going to have a couple of Camorra heavyweights there when we tell him. That'll convince him," Sandro answered. "They'll be there on the night, too. We might need them if Onorio invites too many idiots."

"Don't go in too hard," Fillide warned. This is a party, remember. We want Onorio and Francesco to be friends, feel they can relax and enjoy it."

"Your courtesans will see to that," Sandro answered, "and if they're like you, they'll quieten the fools. It'd be good if there were more women than men, then they could help each other." Onorio wondered what was happening when Fillide sent a message saying she wanted a meeting and grew more apprehensive when he saw Sandro and a couple of hard men there too.

Fillide picked up on his nervousness and reassured him. "Onorio we have a job for you," she announced. "We want you to host the best party that

Rome's seen for years. It's going to be like Cesare Borgia's Night of the Chestnuts - only better! You can invite five or six friends, and there'll be plenty of women to drop to the floor for the chestnuts. After that, it's up to you." Onorio knew what she meant and smiled. Fillide praised his work on the Palazzo again and told him how pleased they were with their home. But it still didn't feel right to him; it wasn't like her to be so generous. She always had another angle. "Why won't you and Sandro be there? What's that about?" he asked. Fillide wanted to tell him as little as possible but knew she had to open up a little. "Alright, it's not a 'thank you' for you alone. It's also for someone who's been helping us here in Marzio. He doesn't know anything about it, and we want it to be a big surprise. You're the host, and I want you to make him feel welcome. Don't worry, we'll arrive later. That's part of the surprise. Now, can you do that for us?"

Onorio nodded, he definitely had the feeling he was being set up but knew it wouldn't be wise to turn her down. "One more very important thing," Fillide added. "Don't invite your friends 'til the last minute, and don't go spreading the news everywhere. We want it to be a surprise, don't we Sandro?"

"These things get out of hand if too many people find out," Sandro said, "so don't tell everyone. Five friends at most and only when we give you the word. If I hear rumours about a big party and your name is mentioned, you're in big trouble." As he said the last words, Sandro glanced at the men from the Camorra. They stared hard at Onorio, and one made a throat-slitting gesture. Onorio's fears were confirmed. This was no party. He was involved in another of Fillide's schemes.

Cassandra Stampa was a friend of Fillide's from their days when they'd been part-time models for the artist Guiseppe Cesare. They'd worked the bars of Marzio together, where they were known for their beauty, heavy drinking and affairs with men who had money. At the same time, they modelled for artists like Titian and Caravaggio - work that won them admirers in prestigious sections of Roman society. As Fillide began to set her trap, she thought of her friend and decided to enlist her. She was exactly the sort of woman Francesco would go for.

As they sat in Fillide's palazzo Cassandra was impressed. "The only way I'll get something like this is by marrying some ugly old fool, and I don't want that," she said. "Not yet anyway, not until I've lost my looks."

Fillide laughed, "Don't worry, that won't happen for a long time and now I want you to help me, I want you to meet someone. He's not old, not too ugly, and he's got money. He also thinks he's God's gift to women. Not so. He needs to be brought down from the clouds." She went on to explain about the Night of the Chestnuts she was organising. "He's trying to cause a lot of problems for Sandro and me, but I want to show people what he's really like - and when I do, no one will listen to him." Fillide didn't tell her the background to the story but explained what she wanted her to do. "We'll find out where he is. He goes around looking for women every night.

When he sees you, he'll be all over you. Tell him about the night and say you'd like to invite him - he can even bring a friend. We want him to be found naked and in a terrible state, disgraced. Then he'll crawl back to where he came from, and we'll have no more trouble with him."

Cassandra had heard stories like this before; revenge and blackmail were regular events in Roman society. She was happy to help, especially when Fillide said there were one thousand scudi in it for her. "I could start tonight," she said. "I know where to find this kind of man." Fillide described him, gave her his name, and told her he was a Knight of Malta. "He's a priest in their order, so he should be celibate. He comes to Rome to escape from all that. He thinks he's very cultured - an art connoisseur - so maybe don't mention Caravaggio and definitely not me. That will scare him off! He always has money from the Church, so good luck, and tell me as soon as you have him hooked."

Afterwards, Fillide carried on making the rest of the preparations. She was confident Cassandra would deliver. But there was one more important part of the night Fillide had to establish. She wanted to make sure Cardinal Baronius found out about the life Francesco was leading but she couldn't compromise him. The less he knew, the safer he'd be. Some members of the College of Cardinals were already suspicious of his involvement with Marzio.

She'd been told that in days gone by, Father Bianchi had visited Marzio as a customer, not a priest, so she decided to involve him. "Father, we may be able to solve the problem of Paulo Francesco and his lying tongue," she told him. "But first I want to ask you a question. If he, a man of the cloth were to be discovered, naked with many whores at a sinful, debauched party, he wouldn't be considered a suitable person to have an audience with His Holiness the Pope, would he?"

Father Bianchi smiled to himself but decided to keep her guessing. "All sinners are welcome in the Church when they ask for forgiveness. You should know that Fillide."

"Of course, but he isn't a sincere person, and he only wants to see the Pope so he can tell more lies," she said calmly. "That can't be right, can it?"

"If something like that happened, I'm sure Cardinal Baronius would know what to do," he replied. "If you told me and you could prove what you were saying - show me the evidence - I'd report everything to him." That was more like it. They understood each other, and Fillide said he'd be the first to know. As she left the Vatican, she felt her plans were coming together. Even so, she knew the plan was full of risk and in a rare moment of doubt she crossed herself, there were anxious days ahead.

Philip E. Rowson

"You are made for Rome, and Rome is made for you"
Pope Urban VIII to Gian Lorenzo Bernini

Francesco was enjoying his time in Rome as he waited for Baronius to arrange his audience with the Pope. He wasn't hopeful, but one night he was introduced to Bernini who was enjoying his reputation as the 'Pope's favourite architect.' He told everyone that the Pope had commissioned him to 'change the face of Rome,' and he'd recently completed his work on the Piazza San Pietro. This had transformed a previously irregular shape into a commanding introduction to St Peter's Basilica. The square was in perfect harmony with its surroundings yet built on a massive scale.

This was one Bernini's most spectacular achievements. Eager to impress the great man, Francesco praised the square and mentioned that he knew Rubens, who was collaborating with the architect on much of the rebuilding work. "Yes, that's at the command of Pope Urban," Bernini informed him. "It's only a minor role but important to the Pope," the gifted yet egotistical architect was determined not to share the credit.

"I should have been working with Caravaggio, but there were difficulties." That gave the Knight of Malta a chance to boast that he too had encountered Caravaggio, though he didn't explain why he was in Rome. As the night went on, they got more friendly and boisterous as Francesco ordered more and more wine. Bernini was in the mood to relax. His work was receiving praise from all sides, and the Pope had promised bigger budgets to come. Spotting a couple of courtesans, he invited them to join their company. One of them was Cassandra Stampa. Bernini was well known in Rome, and he made the introductions. When he said, "And this is Paulo Francesco, a Knight of Malta," Cassandra's smile became instantly more welcoming. From then on, he had her full attention, which he found intensely satisfying. Cassandra thought Fillide had summed him up well; he was very full of himself. She didn't have to make conversation, simply listening kept him happy.

When she could see Bernini getting bored she changed the subject towards his work for a while. The art of the courtesan wasn't limited to the bedroom. "Your Piazza San Pietro is a masterpiece," she said. "You're a great artist too, but so much better looking in the flesh than in your self-portrait." Cassandra knew how to lay it on thick and still sound sincere. She had both of them dancing frantically to her tune. They enjoyed the night tremendously and Francesco was desperate to take her to bed. Cassandra gently put him off. She had him and he'd have to wait.

Philip E. Rowson

Jealousy and rage in a night that went too far

"Don't worry, he'll be there - his tongue was hanging out," Cassandra said after describing her encounter with Francesco to Fillide. When she said she'd met Bernini too, Fillide told her to bring him along. "He's very important in Rome, he'll make it even more of an occasion."

"We're all set," she told Sandro later. "Onorio knows it's tomorrow night, the women are ready, and I've ordered food." Fiammetta Michaelis, the lover of Cesare Borgia, had agreed to rent her house on Via dei Coronari to them for the night. "She was very interested when I told her we were holding a Night of the Chestnuts." Sandro scowled at that, he wasn't by anything the Roman Aristocracy might say. "She's even more interested in the money we're paying," he said contemptuously. "From what I hear she'd be happy to join in with the courtesans."

Fillide discreetly warned Father Bianchi that, "Something may happen tonight." He sighed and resolved to wait, he knew Fillide was planning something and wanted him involved. Sandro briefed his Camorra heavyweights. He told them this was work, even though they'd be at a party. "You can join in and enjoy yourselves but be ready." Shaking his head, he told them he couldn't believe he was paying them for this. "Well, someone's got to do it," they replied.

Onorio could hardly believe it either. He'd limited himself to just four friends who were delighted to accept - slightly puzzled too, though they weren't about to let that hold them back. As the host, Onorio welcomed Francesco and Bernini when they arrived with Cassandra. He bowed to Francesco and told him loudly, "You sir, as a Knight of Malta, will be the guest of honour. It will be my duty to make sure you enjoy the night." Francesco loved that, imagining it would impress Cassandra. 'If only he knew,' she thought to herself, smiling sweetly. She'd already decided Bernini was the prize of the night and meant to capture him.

Swallowing his professional pride, Onorio also praised Bernini as "The architect who will make Rome the envy of the world again." It was a good move. Bernini loved flattery and pretended to have forgotten the way he'd dismissed Onorio months earlier. "That's good to hear from a distinguished architect like yourself," he said grandly. Before long, everyone was getting on well together. The courtesans knew they'd be well paid at the end of the night and were doing their job. They greeted all the guests like old friends and lovers. Laughter bubbled away, wine filled every cup, and sex hovered on the fringe of conversation.

The house was built around a large, open area for guests to mingle and meet partners. Dark alcoves for private encounters were tucked away down corridors. To set the mood, musicians played in a room separate from the guests. Once the party started, they were dismissed - no distractions or witnesses were needed. The atmosphere was expectant; everyone knew that soon, social graces would be thrown to one side.

After a few cups of wine, Onorio was more relaxed and into the spirit of the occasion. Calling for silence, he announced, "Tonight is the Night of Chestnuts, and we are in the very room where Cesare Borgia, a man who knows how to enjoy himself, started this tradition. I'm sure everything will go even better this time so let the celebrations begin!"

The courtesans started to dance together to the singing of the men, holding each other around the waist and moving around the edges of the room. Cassandra was in the lead, and after every four or five steps she lifted an arm and they all stopped. That was the signal for them to begin to strip off their clothes, one flimsy garment at a time.

After four stops, they were completely naked and had visited every corner of the room. By this time guests were cheering, and Onorio waved for the courtesans to join him in the centre. They huddled together with Onorio in the middle, and as the excitement built, the men began to chant "Chestnuts, chestnuts!"

With a theatrical gesture Onorio produced a large bag and threw handfulls of chestnuts in the air.

It was the beginning of a wild sight with courtesans rushing in every direction, playfully pushing and shoving each other as they fought for the nuts on the floor.

Once they'd got one they got down on hands and knees to eat. The erotic sight was the signal for the men to join in and soon there were couples, threesomes, and foursomes all over the floor.

It was mixed wrestling, loud and hot, with every hold allowed as partners moved on - or shared.

Francesco had made an instant grab for Cassandra and wouldn't be separated from her. She went along with his wild lovemaking for a while then managed to slip free telling him, "Enough, enough!"

Filling a wine cup, she gave it to him and, moving away, began talking to one of Sandro's Camorra heavies, Roberto Fabiola. He was resting after his first 'encounter,' and casually asked how well she knew Francesco. "Not very well," she replied. "We came together, and he thinks I'm the one for him, but I don't agree."

"Well, he might not see it your way," Roberto said, watching Francesco approach. Sandro had told him if there was any drama, it would probably be around Francesco. "Don't let him start anything, he's got a temper when he's drinking. We have business with him later so keep him safe."

He couldn't spell out what they had in mind because he didn't know how the night would go - and neither did Fillide. That made her nervous; she always wanted control. They were watching together from an upstairs room through a secret spy hole. From there they could see most of what was happening, and sure enough, Francesco made his move. "This one's special," he said. "She's with me."

Roberto shrugged, "I don't think it works that way, everyone is with everyone." That didn't suit the eager Francesco, " Who says that?" he demanded, "We're together."

"Whatever you say," Roberto let it go. He was staying calm, following instructions. Upstairs Fillide said, "Did you see that? He's going to be trouble." "What do we do?" Sandro asked. Fillide didn't know herself yet. "I want him to get really drunk so we can call Father Bianchi and show him what a stupid fool he is. I have a potion that will help."

Sandro said he'd give it to Roberto and tell him to slip it into Francesco's wine. Taking care not to be seen, he went downstairs and spoke to Roberto. "Put this in his wine and stay close. It should make him pass out."

Even in all his party going days, Onorio had never had a night like this. He'd forgotten he was meant to be the host and take care of Francesco. He was happy, busy with courtesans and Bernini was doing the same. At that moment he was engrossed with Cassandra and Francesco wasn't happy. He was just about to pull her off him when Roberto stopped him.

"Let him enjoy, you'll be next," he promised. " Here, have a drink." He stood between Francesco and Cassandra and there was no way Francesco was getting past him.

To save face Francesco grabbed the wine and took a deep gulp. "Just enjoy the night," Roberto suggested calmly. "There's plenty more beautiful women and fine wine too, nothing but the best for you my friend."

As the wine began to affect him Francesco grunted in agreement and moved away. Roberto followed him and put a friendly arm around his shoulder, steering him towards a couch.

All around them the party was getting louder and more extreme as guests and courtesans lost all their inhibitions and indulged themselves in a frenzy of feral coupling.

Most of the men had stripped off too and were enjoying the attention of two, sometimes three women. Some women were pairing off together as men watched and applauded therir efforts. A drunk friend of Onorio's told him, "At Cesare Borgia's Night of the Chestnuts, he handed out prizes for the best performance. Are you going to? You have to, you're the host," he insisted.

Onorio didn't have any prizes and in any case he was past caring about his duties as a host. "Later, later," he announced. "But don't get too excited, I'll give myself first prize."

"Or maybe I'll give it to those two," he laughed pointing to two women making love on a couch. "Come on let's join them."

Watching the orgy from above, Fillide and Sandro had seen Roberto dropping a potion into the wine before handing it to Francesco. It wasn't long before the guest of honour fell asleep on the couch and flopped onto his side snoring loudly.

Everything was going according to plan until Onorio eventually moved on from his foursome and saw Francesco sleeping. Suddenly remembering he was supposed to make sure the guest of honour had a good time, he shook him vigorously. "Wake up, wake up! The night's only just beginning, you're missing everything."

Francesco came round and struggled to get up. His first thought was of Cassandra. "Where's Cassandra, where's Cassandra?" he asked desperately. "The one I came with; she's mine!" Onorio could see that he was agitated and drunk: a dangerous combination. It didn't help when he looked around and couldn't see Cassandra. "Where is she?" he demanded. Onorio knew he'd have to act because Francesco was causing a scene. "Don't worry, I know where she is," he lied but Roberto arrived and came to his rescue.

"My friend, all is well," he said, hugging Francesco tightly to his chest. "I just saw her and she was asking for you. Just wait here and gather your strength. You'll need it," he laughed. "I'll bring her right now." He darted off, muttering to Onorio to stay with him.

The evening sun had faded, and the only light was from flickering candles high up on the chandeliers. There were naked couples everywhere, and Roberto wasn't inclined to go round making close inspections; that invited certain trouble. He had a strong suspicion Cassandra would be with Bernini. Sure enough, he found them locked together, and this time he pulled Bernini away saying, "Excuse me sir, I need this woman."

The architect saw Roberto's bulk and didn't protest. Grabbing hold of Cassandra's wrists he dragged her away, hissing "Come with me. Francesco's looking for you."

Cassandra was no stranger to rough treatment at Roman parties and knew it wasn't wise to protest. She also saw the lion's head ring on his right hand and recognised it as a Camorra sign of high rank. She didn't struggle and suggestively snuggled up to him instead, murmering, "Can't I stay with you? It could be good." Thinking it would help to keep her away from Bernini, Roberto let her kiss him.

It was a mistake; she wasn't about to let him go, and he didn't feel inclined to struggle - until Francesco saw them. He'd angrily stormed away from Onorio, cursing him, blaming him because Cassandra wasn't there. As he wandered round the love-making couples frantically searching his anger and frustration gave him a surge of energy.

The second he saw them he flung himself at Roberto, arms flailing. Roberto was knocked off balance and they fought wildly on the floor. He'd been taken by surprise at the strength of the attack but there was only going to be one winner and Francesco knew it. Mad with rage, he pulled a knife and stabbed the Camorra hardman in the arm.

He was raising the knife for a second blow when Bernini acted. Moving with the speed of a much younger man, he grabbed Francesco's arm, and the knife dropped to the floor. Then, as Bernini and Francesco struggled to reach the knife, Cassandra saw her chance. Snatching the knife away from them, she stabbed Francesco in the stomach, sinking the blade in up to the hilt.

As he gasped and staggered back, she pulled the knife out and stabbed again. Fatally this time, under the heart.

Like Fillide she'd been brought up in a tough school. After the first wound you had to finish – or be finished.

Two months later, Fillide and Sandro were relaxing in a villa in Sicily. Looking back at the year just gone, Fillide thought she could never, even if she lived through centuries of Roman history, plan a night with such a viciously perfect ending as that.

When she got to the scene of the stabbing Francesco was dead, Cassandra was in shock, and Bernini was desperately trying to stop the blood flowing from Roberto's arm. Sandro reacted first, announcing to all the guests, "I am Sandro Tomassoni, Capo di Marzio. There's been an accident, but please stay calm and in the house. There's plenty of food and wine if you want it. We'll take care of everything, no need to panic."

Roberto's wound wasn't serious, and his Camorra comrade bound it up before helping Sandro to reassure the guests again. Most of them began looking for their clothes and got dressed. Some reluctantly but most of the courtesans were happy to leave, they knew they could be dragged into the affair if they hung around. It wasn't unusual for nights like this to end with a stabbing and when they did the Papal Guard was likely to blame them.

Fillide didn't have any worries like that and she stayed by the body, comforting Cassandra, promising she would be protected. "You aren't going to end up in court over this. It will all be covered up. He has no standing in Rome, he will be forgotten."

She said the same thing to Bernini, assuring him his name would be kept out of the whole affair. "Someone from Cardinal Baronius's office will be here soon to take care of everything." She'd already sent for Father Bianchi, saying there'd been an accident and that he should come straight away.

When he arrived with a Commander from the Papal Guard, she explained that Francesco had been drunk and violent and tried to kill a guest. He'd been killed in self-defence, but she wouldn't say who'd done it. When Bianchi saw Bernini his first thought was 'She's done it this time, now the Pope could be involved.'

He ordered Sandro to cover Francesco's body and take it away. "Keep it somewhere safe 'til we decide what to do." Bianchi's priority was Bernini. If anything happened to upset him, or if rumours about him being involved in a murder started, the

Pope would hear about it and there'd be endless complications.

He knew Baronius would see it that way too. Taking Bernini to one side, he said, "Nothing that happened here concerns you. There's no reason for you to be involved in any way. I'm speaking for Cardinal Baronius; I can promise you that. As an important citizen of Rome, you are under the protection of Pope Urban. The Guard Commander will escort you home now, and it would be best if you didn't talk about this again."

The only thing Bernini wanted was to get away, so he agreed but stopped to console Cassandra before he left. "Don't worry, you'll be alright. I'll come and see you soon." She hoped that was true. After he'd gone, Fillide hugged her, saying, "I think he means it, I could tell." She'd no idea whether he would or not, but Cassandra needed to hear that - she was still shaking.

As the guests started to leave, Bianchi told Fillide, "We have to keep this quiet. It didn't happen. At noon today, you will see Cardinal Baronius and tell him everything. I mean everything. I've no idea how you arranged this very convenient death - with Bernini as a witness - but I know you did."

The death of Francesco was managed so well that Roman society never did find out there'd been another Night of the Chestnuts. A relieved Cardinal

Baronius was able to tell the Knights of Malta their man had died in scandalous circumstances, and they'd be wise not to investigate. Best of all, the Pope didn't get involved, and Bernini carried out his work uninterrupted. He did see Cassandra again; she became his mistress, and to her delight, he built her a house even grander than Fillide's. When everything was finally laid to rest, Baronius called Fillide to a meeting. "I think it's time you and Sandro left Rome for a while. You've had too many 'accidents' lately. I'll find someone to take over Marzio while you're away."

Fillide looked upset at this news, but Baronius had more to say. "I've had some interesting enquiries about both of you from Sicily. I think you should go there." He told her that 'certain people' had been impressed by the protection scheme they'd set up in Marzio. "These people think it would work well - and be mutually beneficial - in Sicily." Baronius tapped the side of his nose in the age-old sign for confidentiality. "They say they need someone with experience who's totally ruthless. For some reason, I think that sounds like you and Sandro. I've spoken to the Pope's treasurer and explained how it could help the work of the Church in Sicily. I also said if it was successful, we'd make a profit. So, we're prepared to invest to help you set up a protezione. Do you agree?"

Fillide didn't hesitate. Her only question was "When do we go?" "Tomorrow, to a little place called Corleone," Baronius replied. "They'll be waiting for you."

Sandro finds Sicily to his liking

The two Roman exiles found themselves at home in Sicily. When they arrived in the capital of Palermo, they were given a stylish Palazzo near the town centre to stay in while they looked around. Stories of their takeover of Marzio had impressed the patriarch of a powerful Sicilian family, Salvatore Randazzo, and he was responsible for their invitation to the island.

His reasons were simple. The patriarch was disappointed in his two sons who he'd decided had neither the talent nor the determination to build the family business, and that grieved him. He'd had long discussions with his consigliere, Gian Mariano, and they'd agreed it was at least worth a try. "Let's see if these smart citizens from Marzio can handle life in Sicily. We've got nothing to lose. They can always go back home crying if it doesn't work."

He brought Mariano to the important first meeting with Fillide and Sandro and began to lay out the situation. "The opportunities are all around us here, but everyone is too interested in fighting each other. Unfortunately, my sons can't see what's in front of their eyes. When Cardinal Baronius spoke to me, I began to think maybe you could succeed here. But then, I asked myself, why would you come? "Then the Cardinal tells me your story, explains why you have to leave Rome. I enjoyed that: the way you went about your business. Now, this is your opportunity. Think of Sicily as a bigger Marzio with five times as much to offer - but without people like the Pope, the Vatican and the College of Cardinals looking over your shoulder. Think what you can do with that."

Fillide was intrigued. She could tell by the way Randazzo spoke that his motivation was deep frustration. It was hard for a man like him to dismiss his sons. On the other hand she was sure he was offering the opportunity to Sandro, and she wasn't about to swap one set of problems for another.

All her life she'd been exploited, struggling with men like the Tomassoni brothers; maybe this Randazzo was just another one of the same type of man. Even though she was higher up the power ratings now, this was still a macho world. Randazzo talked almost exclusively to Sandro, doing nothing more than throwing an occasional glance in her direction. Sandro listened with his head down, lifting it occasionally to acknowledge Randazzo but not giving anything away. Even Fillide couldn't work out what he was thinking. When she'd come back from her meeting at the Vatican, Sandro expected her to say they'd caused too many problems and they had to leave. He was prepared for that: above all, he was a realist - but also an optimist. They'd come through a dangerous series of situations and made more money than he'd seen in his life. His thoughts about the future had begun to drift towards Naples and his connections there.

When she told him about the offer to go to Sicily, he could hardly believe it and looked at Fillide with even more respect. He knew an opportunity like that wouldn't be offered to him. In some ways, his pride was hurt, but he accepted it was her thinking and attitudes that made the difference. He couldn't scheme and persuade like her; even a difficult man like Caravaggio accepted her, and Paulo Francesco had lost his mind over her.

More to the point, he realised important people in the Vatican appreciated what she could bring to the table. But right now, he was beginning to feel uncomfortable about the way the talk was directed solely at him, leaving Fillide out.

He knew she'd be fuming; it was just a matter of time before she spoke out, and he was certain their hosts would be offended. Then came a surprise. Turning to Fillide, Randazzo said, "The Cardinal tells me you have a certain way of approaching situations and overcoming difficulties, twisting events so they work to your advantage. That's a skill we need here."

Pleased that he was making an effort to include her, Fillide responded quickly. "The Cardinal's been a good friend to us; we try to think what would work best on his side of the table as well as ours. Then we make our plans - Sandro and I work together." She'd accepted the compliment and made her point that this was a partnership. But in her mind, she kept coming back to the money. She'd been so surprised and flattered by the trust Baronius had shown that she'd simply said yes without thinking it through. She was also afraid he might withdraw the offer if she raised difficulties or followed her usual instincts and tried to haggle with him. But haggle about what?

This was another world she was stepping into. She'd no idea how much work they'd need to do to set something up - or whether they'd even live to enjoy it. And what was that Randazzo said about no interference from the Church? Had Baronius given him some sort of guarantee she didn't know about? Ever since she'd started dealing with the Cardinal, she'd been struck by how deeply the Church was involved with the contrasting sides of Roman life: from charity work with the poor to keeping the peace in a red-light district like Marzio. There were constant military campaigns fighting the enemies of Rome; finally the Church supported artists like Caravaggio and architects like Bernini.

So what kind of situation had led to one of the Vatican's most senior Cardinals sitting down with the Treasurer and deciding to invest in a Sicilian Mafioso? All she could come up with was that the power struggle inside the Vatican was never far from the mind of men like Baronius. Was the new Pope so insecure that he was looking for allies and money wherever he could find them, even in a wild and lawless Sicily? "We've heard good things about your partnership," Randazzo continued looking from one to the other, including them both. "The way you set up your scheme in Marzio with suppliers and traders so that they paid you to settle disputes between them. Like I said, here in Sicily we fight each other all the time. Your way, we get paid from both sides. That only works if you are strong enough, but we can make sure you are."

He ended by looking directly at Sandro who didn't change his expression. He wasn't ready to jump into the discussion yet.

Fillide was more than ready. "That's the way we operated, but there's more to it. The poor in Marzio came out better too. It's a simple idea: the Cardinal came to us because there was no peace in Marzio. People were afraid to be on the street, scared of being robbed for food, killed for the clothes they stood up in. When people have nothing, they're desperate - so we used some of the money to help them, and things started to change. People felt safe, trade improved. Life in Marzio was better, and we still made money for ourselves. But it's not easy, I promise you."

Randazzo was silent for a moment, shocked. This wasn't in his thinking; his plans didn't include helping the poor. "In Sicily, we leave charity to the Church; that's their business. We take care of our own families, and to do that you have to be strong. And isn't it true that many people died while you were keeping the peace?"

"That's true," Sandro said, speaking for the first time, "but they were people who deserved to die. My uncles did bad things in Marzio. My uncle Giovanni was Capo, but he never should have been. He came for us, so we killed him and his guards. They had to go. Then the Knights of Malta came for us. We killed them too. After that, people listened to us, able to see how we make things better, not worse. Of course, we made money because we deserved to. It would never have happened if we'd been like my uncles. Everyone would still be fighting and killing each other." There was silence again as Randazzo and Mariano considered what they'd heard.

Mariano spoke first. "I think our position would be that you can do whatever you like with your share. Help the poor, invest in land; it's cheap in Sicily compared to Rome - that's for you to decide. But we take our share first." There was another silence, then Fillide spoke. "Naturally we have to agree between ourselves who gets what. If we're doing the work - starting the business and running it - we expect the biggest share."

"We're getting too far ahead," Randazzo answered quickly. "If we're working together, we must agree, but first we have to get to know each other, and you need to learn about Sicily."

By now he'd seen how they worked together and realised it was Fillide he'd have to negotiate with. Sandro would probably prefer not to negotiate at all - or with a knife in his hand. There was nothing special about that, he was used to it. These were early days.

Fillide and Sandro discovered that as they moved around the island, they only needed to mention the name of Randazzo, and they were offered hospitality and advice about which farmers, landowners and merchants they should visit, and others they should be wary of. Randazzo said he'd provide escorts for them, but usually, they preferred to go alone and see for themselves.

That approach nearly ended in disaster. One day, they were stopped by three men who questioned them aggressively, asking who they were and why they were there. When Sandro mentioned Randazzo, the atmosphere grew darker, and he thought they were going to be attacked. Putting his hand on his knife, showing them he was ready to fight, he tried to reason with them. Fillide could see it wasn't going well and started to shout "Veniamo derubati!" – 'We're being robbed'.

A woman came rushing out from where she'd been working in a field and, taking in the scene, quickly started to wave her arms and shout abuse at the men with many mentions of Don Randazzo. They backed off and went their way. The woman introduced herself as the farmer's wife and said, "I know who you are: you are the guests of Don Randazzo and should be treated with respect. These men will suffer for what they did." That night they were visited by Gian Mariano who apologized. "They were strangers from another part of Sicily. They shouldn't have been there, and they've been dealt with. Because of this, Don Randazzo will make sure that two Soldati are always with you. You won't be troubled again."

Afterwards, Sandro told Fillide there was a fatal flaw in this solution. "They'll always be Randazzo's men. I need men to guard my back, not soldiers with divided loyalties. We should look to bring some of our people down from Rome." Fillide said nothing, she sensed they could easily offend their new colleagues if they showed, in such an obvious way, that they didn't trust them. For the moment, she suggested they set up meetings in their Palazzo in Palermo. "Let's get some merchants to come and talk to us - get something started. Then we can tell Randazzo it's better to have some of our own people."

Sandro could see the sense in that. "Maybe I can get close to a couple of Randazzo's guards - get them to show me the bars on market days."

"That's what you do best Sandro," Fillide said. "Be their friend. Don't always think they're looking to stab you in the back."

"We're in Sicily, not Marzio," he warned her. "I'll be friendly. You know what they say here: keep the people you like close. Keep the ones you don't closer." Fillide smiled. "Spoken like a Mafioso Sandro, getting there. We can make this problem go away"

Randazzo introduced Fillide and Sandro to a few local traders and described how they'd taken hold of a tough area like Marzio, but Fillide knew they wouldn't make any real progress until she had a good pitch ready. The story of how Sandro had taken control at the point of a sword was noted, but even though they had the backing of Randazzo, they came from a world the Sicilians had no reason to trust. It didn't worry her too much; she was confident that after a few early victories word would get around and they'd be in business.

She also began to see why Randazzo needed them; there was bad feeling in the air.

Together with his sons, he'd been involved in too many disputes in the past. Blood was spilt, money lost, and trust was hard to rebuild. Fear had given him a dominant position, but even that was under constant threat, and the relationships he had built weren't stable. The opportunity for somebody new to come in and deal with both sides was there. But without their own power base, Sandro and Fillide had no credibility. Randazzo was no more than an introduction.

"We have to contact Baronius," Fillide told Sandro, "or go and see him. He said the Church would invest in us and now's the time. We need funds."

"Go and see him," Sandro said immediately. "Get the money and bring Aldati and Troppa back with you. You'll need them as protection anyway, in Sicily there's danger everywhere. And when we get started, I want them and at least five more like them at my back. I trust Aldati to find the right ones."

Fillide calculated her trip would take at least a month: the longest she'd been away from Sandro since they'd got together. "Maybe we should both go," she suggested to him, but he was against it. "Baronius doesn't want to see me; it's you he trusts. He thinks I just cause trouble and kill people."

Fillide accepted that. She knew Baronius was wary of Sandro's aggression and readiness to kill. Before they'd set off for Sicily, he cautioned her. "One day, Sandro will go too far and attack the wrong person. It's a mistake that could be the end of him. You must be in his ear, all the time, or you'll go with him. He's not a bad person, but he doesn't think ahead. That's what you must do, Fillide: think for him. If you do, you can go far." She knew it was good advice, but easier said than done, especially when she wasn't there. They told Randazzo what they planned to do, and he said he'd go with her: there were people he had to see. He'd first heard about Fillide and Sandro and their work on a trip to Rome when he was trying to set up supply lines. A friend told him Cardinal Baronius was a good contact so he asked to see him, saying he was looking for advice about trading. Sensing there might be a chance for the Vatican to gain some influence in Sicily, Baronius had introduced Randazzo to a trader who operated from Marzio and worked with Fillide and Sandro.

The trader told Randazzo he kept having trouble with local bars. "They wanted produce and wine, but they were slow to pay, always trying to cheat me. Even though It would have hurt my business I was going to stop trading with them. But I paid Fillide instead. Sandro and his men went to see them, and now they pay up on time." He laughed, "Believe me, nobody wants trouble with Sandro and his men."

Baronius told him there were other traders with stories like that, and if he wanted to set up a similar scheme in Sicily, he might be able to help. "That's the best advice I can give you," he said as Randazzo left. "Come back and see me soon. You'll be helping yourself, Sicily and His Holiness the Pope."

After the Night of the Chestnuts episode and the trouble Fillide and Sandro were in, Baronius remembered the conversation. The Pope was being attacked by the College of Cardinals for what they saw as his lavish spending on the rebuilding of Rome. Bringing Sicily closer to Vatican control without an expensive military campaign would deflect some of the criticism. When he talked the idea through with Bianchi, another thought came to him. "Just imagine that: if Fillide and Sandro do go to Sicily they'll be Ambassadors for Rome and the Pope."

"That's a strange way of thinking, crazy or genius," Bianchi replied. "I don't know which."

"Could be both. I've heard Fillide's on her way to see me. I guess we'll soon find out."

On the trip from Sicily to Rome, Fillide heard from Randazzo what happened when he met Baronius. "He had many good things to say about you and Sandro." Later she worked out that it must have been well before the Night of the Chestnuts, so the Cardinal may have been planning something all along.

She'd wondered about that; the offer was made so quickly when they were in trouble. Either way, she didn't mind, Sicily was an opportunity she was going to grab. When she sat down with

Baronius, she couldn't resist bringing up the timing. "Randazzo told me you talked about us with him a long time before we went to Sicily. And he said you told him what we're planning could help the Pope. I don't understand - how do we fit into all this?"

Baronius decided he'd have to get her more involved if he was going to get the best out of her. "Fillide, you need to start thinking in a different way: a bigger way. This isn't just about a few farmers and merchants in Sicily. The Pope has to look beyond the holy life. He has to think about the material needs of the Church. Finance: how we keep money coming in, how we control what goes out." He stopped. He could see Fillide was still wondering what this had to do with her, so he began to explain his motivation.

"When Rome goes to war with other Italian states, there's a price to pay; wars are expensive. When we're victorious, money comes back to the Church. Many other times, it doesn't, so we have to try and work with our enemies instead. We trade with them, offer to help. That's where you and your scheme come in. Men like Randazzo benefit so there's more trade between Sicily and Rome. Naturally, the Vatican benefits, merchants here in Rome benefit, and there's more money to pay wages. You and Sandro collect too." Baronius waited for her to take that in.

"You're privileged," he told her. "You have a seat at the table where important matters are decided. No other woman from Marzio has ever had that position. You should appreciate it, act wisely, make the most of it." She hadn't expected anything like this: for him to be so open. He'd been using her, she could see that, but she didn't mind. Usually, women had to be born into the right family to get an opportunity like this.

Even then it was rare, and only ever came through a husband or lover. "Thank you for being honest with me," she said and thought back guiltily to the lies she'd told him about the murder of Caravaggio and the trap she'd set for Francesco.

Baronius seemed to have read her mind. "In future, you have to be more honest with me," he said firmly. "I'll always find the truth anyway, you know that, but I want to be able to trust you. We'll both hear plenty of lies as we go forward, but I promise you won't hear any from me."

Fillide nodded in gratitude, "Nor from me." She could hardly speak. He'd been more honest with her than any other man she'd ever met. She moved on to give him an account of what had happened so far in Sicily and why she thought they'd succeed. "It makes sense: they win and we win. I'll prove it and they'll be back for more. But we need money to set up our organisation and we need good men - strong men. Sandro said we need at least seven from Marzio, and we'll recruit some locals too. hirst He wants to bring in Giancarlo Aldati who worked with us in Marzio. Sandro trusts him to find the kind of people he needs. "But most of all we need funds. I have to go back with a chest of money."

"You'll have it," Baronius told her. "I always planned to invest in this idea. I've had to go right to the top: meetings with the Treasurer of the Vatican Bank, His Holiness the Pope himself. I had to convince them this scheme would work. I told them all about what happened in Marzio."

Fillide couldn't help but gasp at that. Did the Pope know what happened? "Not everything or you wouldn't be sitting here now. Just the good parts. They know you helped to change Marzio from a scandalous, lawless place into something better. The Church can't approve of places like Marzio, but the Pope calls it a necessary evil. He says Sicily is different. Many people support the Church, but they're poor. If Sicily starts to prosper and their life changes, the Church will be happy. He prays for your success and waits for good news."

The meeting was over, but Baronius left her in doubt about the importance of what was happening. "Big changes have to start somewhere, and this one starts with you and Sandro," he said. "The Vatican needs to see that Sicily can change: come closer to Rome, closer to becoming a Papal state. That will be the return on their investment. And just like every other business transaction, they want to see a return. My name is on this deal. So is yours and so is Sandro's."

Then, before he left, he turned to deliver the biggest surprise of all. "The Pope agreed there could be a budget of five thousand scudi. Only the three of us and the Vatican Bank know that. Keep it that way, and you'll have more chance of getting out of Sicily alive."

After she left Baronius, Fillide went straight to her palazzo in Marzio. A friend had moved in to look after it, and she was pleased to see everything was as she left it. The new Capo appointed by Baronius had taken on Giancarlo Aldati, and he was keeping an eye on her pride and joy. "Welcome back to Rome." He greeted her warmly and gave an account of everything that had happened since she left. It turned out to be 'not much,' so when she explained that Sandro needed him again, he was delighted.

"Sicily, yes!" he exclaimed. "I had good times with the Legion in Sicily before we crossed the sea to conquer the land of the Pyramids. It'll be good to go back; life's been too quiet in Marzio." Then he remembered one unusual visit. "Cesare Borgia came. He wanted to hear all about your Night of Chestnuts. He kept boasting about his, so I said yours was a lot quieter, that you weren't even there, and it was just a sort of... party night. I don't think he believed me. I think he must have heard about Francesco. I said nothing, but then he wanted to know where you were now, and I just said you'd gone off to the country. He's a wild man, but they say he's won victories with his army and that his father will be Pope one day."

Fillide made no comment. Her conversation with Baronius had opened her eyes to the way power flowed through the Vatican, and she had every reason to hope Pope Urban would stay in place for some time to come. "We need to recruit five men to come back to Sicily with us," she said. "Sandro said he wanted fighters he can rely on, and he trusts you to find them. We have a chance to make something good, so think hard and choose well."

"Petronio Troppa will come, and I can find at least four more," he said. "As many as we need - leave it to me." Three days later, he told her he'd signed "Good soldiers; I've served with them. Sandro will be happy." Randazzo stopped by the palazzo to say he was ready to travel back. Then, casually, fishing for information, "I visited Cardinal Baronius in the Vatican. He said you were making progress in Sicily." He looked expectantly at her, but she just nodded and agreed. "We can talk when we get back," she replied in a tone that didn't invite further questioning.

Baronius had warned her not to talk money with him and only take a small amount of cash with her. He planned to set up a banking arrangement for her with the Bishop of Palermo. "I don't want Randazzo to see you coming back from Rome with a treasure chest. It will give him the wrong idea. I'm trusting you to use the money wisely, Fillide. Remember, the Pope himself is praying for you, he wants you to use the judgement I've told him you have."

The next morning, as Fillide and Aldati stood on the quayside waiting to sail back to Sicily, they had a visitor.

"He who is highly esteemed is not easily conspired against"

Nicolo Machiavelli

Cesare Borgia galloped onto the quay at the head of a small troop of soldiers. He was at the height of his fame, fresh from victories in Northern Italy, where he commanded an army of three hundred cavalry and four thousand infantry and won the title of Duke of Romagne. Some considered him the 'most handsome man in Italy,' and contemporary artists used his features in portraits of Christ. Jumping down from his heavily sweating horse, he swaggered up to Fillide. "So, you are Fillide Melandroni: model of Caravaggio, favourite of Cardinal Baronius and Queen of Marzio."

It wasn't a question, there was a mixture of heavy sarcasm and admiration as he looked her up and down. "Some would say you're too slender to be beautiful but not to my eyes. It's a pity you weren't at my Night of Chestnuts. I would have enjoyed it, and so would you." He offered his hand and she reluctantly kissed it, wondering what would happen next. She was relieved he'd referenced Baronius. At least he was aware she wasn't some courtesan he could treat as he pleased. "Flametta Michaelis told me you rented her house," he continued, "for your own Night of the Chestnuts. Did it go well?" Fillide knew it was pointless denying the night even though it was the last thing she wanted to discuss. "Those who went told me it did. I only organised it. I didn't go myself."

"A courtesan who doesn't go to her own parties," he laughed. "You're a mysterious woman, Fillide. I like that. And now you're sailing to Sicily. What interests you there?" He was smiling as he asked, but Fillide sensed the menace flowing towards her. "Cardinal Baronius asked me to go," she answered.

"Baronius sends courtesans to Sicily? Have they none of their own?" he asked in mock surprise. She knew now she was in danger. There was no telling where this conversation was going. Her best chance was to hope he wouldn't interfere with something the Cardinal had arranged.

"My lord, I'm not travelling as a courtesan. Cardinal Baronius has asked me to go on a mission to help the Church and His Holiness Pope Urban." Her cool reply seemed to anger him more. "These Cardinals, they treat the Pope as a fool!" Borgia looked angry now. "Sending courtesans on missions. Do you know how much money the Pope is spending on his works? Fortunes! What would you say if I told you not to go on this foolish mission?"

"I would respectfully ask you to speak with the Cardinal, sir. I go at his bidding." Fillide had no idea how he would react to what was undoubtedly a challenge to someone of high rank, but she wasn't prepared to give in without an argument. To her relief, he reacted calmly, and if he was surprised at the strength of her reply, he didn't show it. Stepping closer and speaking into her ear so nobody else could hear, he said "You have spirit Fillide, I can see that, and I know you're involved in many important matters. Some say it's strange a Cardinal works with a whore from Marzio, but that doesn't trouble me. He has his reasons, hasn't he?"

He stepped back and waited for a reply, but there was nothing she could say. It was just another insult - a reminder of her status compared to him. Then he tried to intimidate her by revealing how much he knew. "Somehow, you're connected to the disappearance of a Knight of Malta, and now you go to Sicily, an island where the Knights are hated. So go there, but when you return, we'll speak again." Smiling slightly to show she meant no offence, but also that she wasn't afraid, she said, "I'll look forward to it, sir."

He continued, charging his words with menace again. "When you return, you may find Cardinal Baronius and the College of Cardinals not so powerful as they were before. They say Rome is the Eternal City, but it's ever-changing, and if you're wise, you'll change with it." All she could think about now was how quickly she could get away. He was playing with her, she knew, but thankfully he moved away, preparing to leave. Then, in a final change of mood, he turned back and teased her gently. "I want to know all your secrets Fillide. Caravaggio's paintings didn't capture the real you. We'll meet when you return. Travel safely."

He rode off leaving her unsettled and desperately trying to guess his intentions. He had the charisma she'd been told about but his threatening tone and predictions about the future weighed more than easy compliments. How did he know so much about her, and why had he come galloping to the quay? Did he really want to stop her, or was it just a part of the power game?

She was allied to Baronius, and in Vatican politics that put her on a different side to Borgia. If his father did become Pope, she could be in trouble. On the other hand, he could have been reaching out to her. Were his last words as friendly as they sounded, or were they really a threat? He was unpredictable, unknowable.

The others were looking at her, waiting for an explanation she couldn't give. Aldati spoke first. "Well done, Fillide, he's not used to people talking back. Everyone has to jump when he speaks."

"I've no idea what that was about," she shouted and began to breathe heavily in delayed shock. "Come on, let's get everything loaded. I want to be miles away, out at sea in case he comes back." Aldati quickly told his men to pick up their bags and get on board. "We sail now," he shouted to the captain as they crossed the gangplank. "Cast off before you find yourself in some Roman jail. Cesare Borgia thinks he's the new Emperor already."

Some of the new recruits who'd never heard of Borgia were told about him and looked at Fillide with respect. So did Randazzo, who was wondering what Borgia had whispered to her. She was a lot more important than he'd first thought.

Sandro was ecstatic when she told him they had the funds to carry out their plans. She followed the advice of Baronius and didn't reveal how much was available, pretending not to know exactly.

"I've found some good men," he said, delivering his news, "Made connections with families, that's what it's all about here. I put bread on the water and the hungry ones came."

Fillide nodded, "And I've brought Giancarlo Aldati and Troppa back with me. Giancarlo's recruited four more: enough to cover your back. You've got what you wanted Sandro; people will listen to us now. We'll have all Sicily working for us!" she boasted. On the long journey back, she'd started to feel better. In Sicily she was far away from the problems of Rome and seeing Sandro again lifted her spirits. He insisted on meeting the new recruits before she had a chance to tell him about Cesare Borgia, but finally, she got him alone and described what happened. "He acted as if he didn't know what we were doing in Sicily, but I'm sure he does. He's cunning."

Sandro's reaction to the story was one of rage and mockery. "What a big man!" he scorned. "Turns up with a troop of soldiers, all to scare one woman. Somebody told him Francesco was stabbed at the party, and there are plenty more stories about how Caravaggio was killed. He'll have heard how we killed my uncle and his guards. We've plenty of enemies ready to blacken our name - that's easy talk. You're close to Baronius so he wants to play the big man against all those red hat Cardinals in the Vatican, he tries to scare you."

Sandro wanted to make her forget all about Cesare Borgia. "That makes him feel good, but he's nothing. And remember, he's got enemies too - big ones. The Vatican will be watching. The Borgias are Spanish, Rome won't like that."

She enjoyed listening to Sandro put forward the other side of the story. He reassured her, pointing out that even if Cesare's father did become Pope, "That changes nothing for us, our life is in our own hands. By the time anyone thinks about us, we'll have made our fortune and we can go anywhere we want. Forget him! If he's as wild as they say, he'll soon be gone. Plenty of important people will want him dead; they're probably getting the poison ready now."

It was typical of Sandro to dismiss Cesare Borgia. He saw things in black and white, no complications. It was obvious to him that anyone who acted like Cesare Borgia would run into more trouble than he could handle. He wouldn't be around long. Pulling her close, he said, "Don't be worrying about Spanish Popes and their mad, illegitimate children. We have other things to do. I haven't seen you for a month. Why are we talking instead of lying in bed, loving each other 'til we're near to death? But that will take a long time, get your clothes off now."

For their first meeting with traders and farmers, Fillide and Sandro arranged a show of hospitality and strength. They appeared together with Randazzo and his consigliere Mariano, but the patriarch's sons and soldiers were nowhere to be seen. Instead, Sandro's men were centre stage, and their appearance made the announcement locals had been told to expect. A new power was in the land. Each man wore a red sash, carried a sword, and looked as if he could easily start - and finish - a fight. But they'd also been instructed by Sandro to 'look friendly and smile.' Their presence made the point well enough.

They had strength, they were organised, and although Randazzo was with them, power had moved on. Fillide chose a small village close to Palermo for the occasion. The village held a market once a week, but today the square was laid out for a people's banquet, Sicilian style. The idea was to impress with power but appeal with generosity. Tables had expensive delicacies specially imported for the occasion as well as local sweets and savouries. Pigs were roasted and there were barrels of Sicilian wine, definitely not Roman; that would have been insulting.

Randazzo made a speech, introducing Fillide and Sandro as "Friends with important contacts. They'll help us trade and work together. Today they invite everyone to break bread with them, eat good food and drink to future." It was an optimistic speech, received mostly in silence. Randazzo had as many enemies as friends in the audience. Some had fought with him and his sons, a few owed him favours, others had grudges grinding away in their memories.

They all shared one sentiment: suspicion towards newcomers. Over the centuries, Sicily had been invaded and ruled by French and Spanish armies, Arabs came from North Africa, British ships sailed in and took what they wanted. The Sicilian response towards them all was to look inwards and build loyalties inside family groups. The family was a defensive wall against outsiders, and disputes with other families would be treated as war.

Peace came slowly, soaked in blood. In this world, Omerta, the ancient word for manhood and masculinity ruled. Fillide understood this. The way of life was similar to her early years in Marzio. She didn't have a family, but she did have Sandro. She'd make sure they were never outsiders; she couldn't allow that. The plan was to integrate: offer a helping hand where needed, brandish a fist where necessary. She'd be the hand, Sandro the fist.

Aldati encouraged his men to mix in with the locals and they worked with farmers for free. Fillide paid the men. She knew their labour would open doors in the future. When a load of grain mysteriously disappeared from a farm where Petronio Troppa was working, he asked around quietly and got two or three suggestions about who'd taken it. Over the next few days, he travelled around with Aldati and a couple of men asking questions, making sure everyone understood that they were going to recover the grain. Word soon spread in the close community, and they were led to a cache of grain that would have been a big loss to the farmer's family. They returned it, and Troppa put out a message.

"We know who did this, and the thief will be dealt with. We'll find him." They did, and he was given a severe beating, though not a fatal one. Just enough for everyone to know that from now on, stealing from your neighbour had serious consequences. Fillide was happy; this was the kind of result she needed. Deeds, not words, would carry the day. Not long afterwards, an unmarried seventeen-yearold girl got pregnant, and the man responsible tried to skip his obligations. Sandro stepped in and told her family. "Leave it to us. He'll pay, one way or another."

The Medicis Move In

Gradually, Fillide and Sandro increased their influence, but it was only after battles with the powerful Florentine Medici family that they really established their position. The Medicis, a branch of the banking dynasty, were using their wealth to create a rural empire in Sicily. They'd begun operating in the east of the island, buying land and moving into farming. Their next move was to gradually control local markets by selling livestock and produce at a loss - but only to begin with. When they had near-monopoly control of the markets, they steadily increased prices. There were riots as villagers tried to grab food for their children, but the Medicis were ready.

They'd brought in mercenaries from Malta who attacked them brutally: men, women and children alike. "Next time, we'll kill you and rape your women," the mercenary leader shouted as the villagers ran for their lives. From then on, every village market was guarded by mercenaries with the Medicis determined to show their power. Fillide knew this was the moment. "We have to move against them now before they get organised and take more land," she told Sandro. "They'll bring in more of their own people from Florence, and the farms will be gone forever. But we can surprise them; they won't be expecting a fight back."

They began by arranging community meetings. At the start of each one, Fillide asked them to be careful about who they talked to. "Watch out for spies," she said mysteriously. That set the tone, creating an angry us-against-them attitude. She said they wanted to hear from them, in their own words, what was happening. As they spoke, they reminded her of proud families who'd come from the countryside to Rome and were struggling to survive. They were naïve, church-going and vulnerable, unfamiliar with the ways of people like the Medicis or the rogues she had to deal with every day in Marzio. "We had our land, we could survive, but sometimes there wasn't enough to eat," one angry farmer told her. "They said we'd be better off working for them, and when you've never had money in your life, that's tempting. They came with sacks of coin, so I sold. Now it's all gone because we can't live on what they pay. They say they'll bring in people from outside if we don't work."

When Fillide stood up and made her call to action, she came straight to the point. "It's no use talking to the Medicis, they're too arrogant to listen. We have to organise and stick together. Sandro and I know what these people are like, and we know how to beat them. You deserve revenge for the way they've attacked you, stolen from you. They think you are simple farmers who know nothing, but you'll be fighting for your land and your children. You'll get your farms back."

To begin with, she could see the scepticism in their faces, and one asked, "Why would you help us? You might be as bad as them." "Yes, we might - but we're not. Ask the people from the villages around Palermo, they'll tell you how we helped them. Our money comes from the Holy Father in Rome, not the richest bank in Florence. That's the difference! And what have you got to lose? You can let the rich bankers cheat you - or join us and fight!"

At times like this, Fillide's emotions always burst through. She'd never mentioned support from the Church before, worried that talk about Rome would antagonise them. After she'd heard about their lives, she knew differently. It was the most powerful appeal she could make. Throughout every meeting, there was an impressive physical force standing directly behind her. Sandro and Aldati were shoulder to shoulder with the men they'd brought from Rome, plus the Sicilians they'd recruited locally. Her audience could see for themselves this was a powerful force. They looked well-armed and capable.

At the end of her appeal, Fillide swung round and introduced Sandro and his men to the audience. "These are the men who are ready to fight. Are you with us?" Carried along by the emotion of the moment the villagers usually joined in and cheered. It was the moment of theatre Fillide had planned; she'd learned how to handle an audience. When Sandro asked for volunteers to fight, he got them.

"The best fortress is to be found in the love of the people"
Nicolo Machiavelli

Sandro and Fillide decided to start the campaign at a village market close to where the Medicis had set up camp. "Our first attack will be the easiest," Sandro said. "We'll have surprise on our side. If we move fast, we can attack again while they're still thinking about what happened." He'd already picked out a second target, a warehouse.

Sandro spent long hours working and training with his men, building their confidence. He was happier than ever that Aldati was with them. His military experience was vital, though at first, he was critical of the latest Sicilian recruits. "They can fight, but they wouldn't last long with the legion. They're farm boys, trained soldiers will cut them to pieces. They need some skills."

He gave them exercises to strengthen their sword arms, eventually choosing a dozen of the strongest to train with the heavy swords they'd bought. But the veteran of many battles told them strength wasn't enough. "Reflexes save lives; speed is as important as strength. You need fast hands." To improve the coordination between hand and eye, he made them practice by fencing with wooden staves. He then fenced against them with a sword, and each time he got close, he put the tip to their ribs saying, "Imagine that cutting into your flesh, through to your lungs. You'll drown in your own blood. Practice!" He took them through the moves: parry and thrust, again and again.

Eventually, he was satisfied they had a chance of surviving battle. "These men will be our first strike force," he told Sandro, "the ones that do the damage." The rest were given heavy clubs and short, armour-piercing daggers. They practised by stabbing into bales of hay as Sandro urged them on. "Dig deep! Imagine you're killing the men from Malta who attacked your women."

In addition to the swords the force had limited firepower. Sandro, Aldati, and Troppa had crude flintlock pistols that took so long to load they could only be used at the start of the battle. But they were valuable for the impact of the sound: the thunder of gunfire would shake the confidence of mercenaries who never expected to face anything more than a handful of surprised and unarmed villagers.

Before the assault, Sandro got everyone together and handed out red sashes. "Red for freedom, red for blood. Compagno d'armi!" At 10 o'clock in the forenoon, as the sun climbed high, they stormed into the market square. Their first volley of fire from the pistols injured two mercenaries. In the panic that followed, the swordsmen ran in and cut down two more. Shouting and cursing, the mercenaries began to fight for their lives, but they were met by the clubs and knives of Sandro's second wave. His supporting troops charged in, lashing out with clubs, hacking at the fallen bodies.

The Medici men were routed. They'd been were relaxed in Sicily, living an easy life and totally unprepared for the speed and aggression of a vicious attack. As soon as they realised what they were facing, they ran. Sandro called a halt when he saw the only ones remaining were the injured who couldn't run.

He didn't want a massacre. "Take their weapons and what food you need, then we go," he told his men. There was no resistance from the watching stallholders; they'd seen the carnage brought by these trained men who arrived in waves of flashing steel. Sandro spoke to calm their fears, reassuring them. "We came for the Medicis, not you. Everyone else is safe. Give the Medicis this message: tell them their time in Sicily is over. They should go back to Florence. We'll attack every day they remain here. Then when we've driven them away, we'll give the land they've stolen back to farmers like you."

He knew that in the coming days, everyone who'd seen this one-sided battle could be a vital ally - even the losers. He knelt by one of the injured mercenaries. "Tell your comrades if they stay, they won't live to spend the money. The men with red sashes are coming for them." His men came away from the fight with nothing more than a few light wounds. They were all on a high, especially those who hadn't been in a battle before. "Stay calm and remember how we won: by keeping our formation," Sandro cautioned. "It won't always be this easy, but well done. We go forward."

He'd been told their next target, a Medici warehouse, would be full of farm produce: grain and vegetables. It was a couple of days march away and news wouldn't have reached it yet - or so he hoped. But that wasn't possible.Their force was thirty strong, and it was impossible to travel through the countryside without being seen or heard. Big groups of armed men were an unusual sight, and, before they'd gone far, a local farmworker saw the chance to make some money - and ingratiate himself with the Medicis.

He raced to where he knew farmers were working, supervised by a Medici mercenary. "An army with swords and guns and wearing red sashes is on the move, marching east," he told Carlo Regio, the man in charge.

It wasn't news he wanted to hear, there'd been rumours of attacks on the Medicis and if they found him he was in trouble. Choosing Vito Conte, the youngest and fastest amongst the workers, he told him, "Run as fast as you can back to the village. It's market day and there'll be mercenaries on duty. Warn them, tell them to send word to the Captain."

When he arrived he saw there was nobody left to take messsage, just the dead and wounded. He spoke to one who was lying in a pool of his blood, "We've been butchered," he groaned. "They came from nowhere, attacked us like wild men." With a sudden spurt of strength he grabbed hold of Vito's arm, "Tell Carlo Regio that Baldassare needs help, tell him I can pay."

Regio listened to Vito's report in alarm. His instinct was to save himself, he wasn't a friend of Baldassare but if he had money, well he was a mercenary. He could take the money then pass on a message. Sure enough when he got to the village he saw Baldassare was near to death and didn't protest as Regio searched him and took his small stache of coin.

When they got news of the slaughter, the Medici command was shaken. Everything had gone to plan so far. They hadn't expected effective resistance but they quickly worked out what might happen next.

"If they're marching East they'll be going for our warehouse in Ragusa. We have to get out there or we'll lose supplies and our winter food."

Without stopping to think who'd organised ther attack they rounded up as many troops as they could find and set off. They were unprepared, disorganised and they made slow progress. Sandro and his men had reached the warehouse well before them, and this time there was no opposition. The warehouse was unguarded, and the farmworkers didn't offer any resistance when Sandro said they were taking over, especially when Fillide explained who they were and what was going to happen. Some of the younger men immediately said they'd fight with them. Aldati looked them over and selected the ones he'd arm. "We'll need them, the Medicis will come in hard," he told Sandro. "And they'll have more artillery."

He posted lookouts on a hill overlooking the track leading to the warehouse, and it was only hours later when the Medici force was spotted. "About twenty men, at least six have muskets," Aldati told Sandro. "They'll be here in an hour."

Once again, Aldati's military training was put to good use, and he suggested a strategy. "We have more men; they have more firepower. We can overcome that if we send ten men to circle round behind them. While they're attacking us here, we come in from the back." Sandro agreed, and Petronio Troppa was sent out with ten of their most experienced fighters to attack from the rear.

"Take two of the pistols," Aldati said, "but don't fire until you hear our shots. Then charge in firing. We'll take them from the front, you come in from the back, and we'll trap them in the middle. Use your clubs, then your blades." He grabbed a knife and pretended to stab Troppa. "We're not taking prisoners."

The battle of Ragusa was the beginning of the end for the Medicis in Sicily, but Sandro's men took heavy losses. The Medicis attacked fiercely, and their muskets killed four men straight away. It wasn't until Sandro's swordsmen got into a rhythm and began to swing their heavy blades that the tide turned. Seeing that they were gradually getting on top, Aldati took five men and broke away from the main battle. Working around the fringes, they chiselled away at the mercenaries in a series of hand-to-hand fights.

Finally, four shots from Troppa and his men broke the spirit of the mercenaries as they were attacked from behind. They heard him shout "Reload!" and attempted to break through the ring of fighters to escape. They had nothing to fight for and most of them threw down their arms and surrendered. The ones who fought on didn't have a chance, Sandro's men were getting a taste for fighting winning battles and the result was another slaughter.

Sandro gathered the survivors together and made them look at their fallen comrades before repeating the speech he'd given earlier. "This is what will happen if we see any of you again. Now go and tell the Medicis it's all over for them. We're taking the land back, they have to leave Sicily."

The Medici Commander, Giulio, was an illegitimate son and not well regarded. He'd been sent to Sicily on trial. "We'll back you with money and soldiers, to begin with, but you have to win your own battles. You can come back a hero – or not at all," his father, Lorenzo Medici told him.

Giulio was ambitious but wary and not grateful for the opportunity. Nothing he'd heard about Sicily encouraged him and he knew that even if he succeeded the bankers in the family wouldn't be impressed. They saw no chance of a return on their investment and that was the only thing that mattered.

"Sicily's a small island ruined by foreign invasion," his older half-brother Francis told him with some satisfaction. There was no way he wanted any part of Giulio's chance of glory.

"Armies come and go, taking what they want then leaving. There's no reason to stay. The people hate you first, then each other. They fight over what's left and wait for the next gang of foreigners. Rome doesn't know what to do with them. They'll fight you to the death. They're a murderous bunch," he continued.

"God be with you," was his final, insincere blessing as Giulio left on his mission. To begin with, Giulio thought he had a chance. He found the locals ready to sell their farms cheaply as soon as he enticed them with sacks of coin. He had no qualms about buying land then selling produce cheap, undercutting the locals.

His soldiers and mercenaries were there to deter opposition - until Fillide and Sandro arrived. It was only when his men were so disastrously defeated that Giulio took seriously an early warning he'd received from the Knights of Malta. The Knights and the Medicis had connections that went back centuries. They were both powerful forces with mutual interests in banking and wars that increased their power. They often worked together, and the Knights had been pleased when they heard the Medicis were taking an interest in Sicily. In the past, the island had been a problem, so they had good reason to worry when they heard about the sudden arrival of the couple from Marzio.

"Nothing good will come of this," said the Knights' Grand Master, Luca Albina. He knew both of them were involved in the death of Francesco and the disappearance of the cash he'd been entrusted with. The Knights wanted revenge, and they didn't trust Rome or Pope Urban VIII.

"Why is Cardinal Baronius, the Pope's righthand man, sending these people to Sicily?" Albina asked at a meeting in Valetta, Malta's capital. "One is a courtesan who seduced Francesco, the other had him killed and robbed him. Yet Baronius and the Pope protect them, then send them where they can harm us."

Aside from their feelings about Fillide and Sandro, the Knights were paranoid about the Pope's intentions in Sicily. The island had always been unsettled. It could easily become a dangerous rogue state - as Giulio saw far too late. He'd been told how the workers at Ragusa changed sides and fought with Sandro's men. One of the soldiers Sandro spared described how he'd been attacked. "They were all around us. It seemed like there were ten of them for every one of us. I was sure I was going to die, then their leader said 'stop.' He put a knife to my throat and said if he ever saw me or any of us again, he'd cut our legs off, put our eyes out, then kill us."

The soldier was trembling as he remembered. Another, older soldier told Giulio, "We were ambushed, they attacked us head on but some got behind. We weren't outnumbered; they were better organised. They fought like a real Roman legion - together."

Giulio listened in horror. He felt guilty. He should have been there with them. But he was desperately out of his depth, only twenty-three with no experience of war. Yet there was arrogance too. He ignored the warning from the Knights of Malta, because after all, 'What could two people, one of them a woman, do?'

He could picture the scene if he went back to Florence. "You were warned and did nothing," his father would say. "Two people defeated you, and all the soldiers we gave you are dead. Where were you? Why didn't you die with your men?" He couldn't face that kind of disgrace, and it wasn't even safe for him in Sicily now. Wondering who could help him to recover, he came up with just one thought. Maybe the Knights of Malta were worried enough about Fillide and Sandro to give him another chance.

He decided to travel to Malta, taking with him a few soldiers who'd stayed loyal to him and the family.

The decisive defeat of the Medicis had sent Fillide and Sandro's reputation soaring into the clouds. The farmers who'd sold their land to the Medicis simply claimed it back. After all, with this new force behind them, who was going to argue?

"Now we move on," Fillide said. "Everyone can see where the power is. We settle disputes, protect farmers and traders. The difference is, now they start paying. We send some money back to Rome, keep what we need, and make sure there's enough left over to help families who need it."

They didn't spell it out to Randazzo like that; they knew they'd have to pay him 'introduction' fees for helping to set the business up, but Fillide could foresee a time when they wouldn't bother. "If we keep on doing what we do best, we won't need him. People will come to us and ask for help."

"You make it sound easy. It isn't," Sandro corrected. "People love us now, they'll do what we say because they're afraid, but then they begin to ask, 'Why should we pay? We don't need them anymore.' So we have to make things a little difficult... Maybe their barn burns down. We have to remind them why they need us. Will they love us then? And will Randazzo just roll over?" Fillide didn't argue. He was right, and she told him so. "Sandro, the only reason we've been successful is because of you and the force you've put together. I know it's not easy and many are against us, but who would have thought we could have come this far?" Sandro smiled in agreement and let it go. "So, I've finally won an argument. Who would have thought that!" Fillide laughed. "We're not arguing! And anyway, we can handle Randazzo. He's not so smart, and all we've done is make his life easier."

Over the next few months, their services grew. They were asked to calm local disputes, mostly over money, and whenever traders from the mainland came, they called to see Fillide. The news that Sicily was a better place to do business had spread, and she was always available, ready to offer advice. If a deal got her approval, it usually went through without hassles, and if it didn't, traders had somewhere to go. Randazzo found that links with the mainland became easier as confidence in trading with Sicily improved. He was reluctant to give them credit when Fillide pointed out how much more business he was doing. When she suggested he should begin to pay for the service that had made it possible, he refused, saying he was the reason they were there, and they were making plenty already. "That's because everyone else pays for what we do. Now it's your turn," she told him. "Surely you can see that." When he continued to argue, Fillide simply shrugged. "That's disappointing. You'll pay, one way or another. Perhaps your new contacts will find you're not so reliable after all when your deliveries don't arrive. They'll ask me why, and I'll say 'why don't you try someone else?' I'll give them a name, and your business with them will be gone forever. Or maybe Sandro will find you're cheating your neighbours here in Sicily and you have to pay them back."

Randazzo went quiet. The reality of what had happened in Sicily hit him, and he didn't know which way to turn. Threaten reprisals? Agree to her terms? Wisely, he didn't argue at that moment. There was thinking to do. Reports about the success of Fillide and Sandro had reached Baronius in Rome. The Vatican's banker in Palermo sent word that Fillide was paying in revenue and already showing a good profit. The Cardinal was pleased, especially after he heard that the Medici family was moving into Sicily. "Competition for them," he said to Bianchi. "This is going to be interesting. The Medicis have sent an illegitimate son to see what he's made of. My guess is Fillide will outwit him, then Sandro will cut his throat."

"Sandro will cut his throat whatever happens," Bianchi replied. "That's the way he is." When they heard that Giulio had fled, Bianchi laughed. "Just in time!" Baronius needed some good news. Pope Urban was worn down by criticism about how much he was spending on restoring the city. "Our mission is to build a kingdom in heaven, not palaces in Rome," was the general gist, and the rise of the German Protestant Martin Luther was worrying the Vatican establishment. Baronius was seen as a key supporter of the Pope, so he decided to take a bold route and speak out. "Rome is the creation of our Church, respected and feared in many lands. If Rome looks weak, so does the Church, and that only helps the Protestants. We have to make Rome great again, the centre of our Catholic Church. The place pilgrims visit and are inspired to go home and spread the word of the Lord."

The Pope was grateful for his intervention, and Baronius had some support in the College of Cardinals, but the arguments continued. Though the money that came in from the pilgrims was welcome, the Spanish Borgia family had their eye on succeeding to the papacy and were ready to bribe their way to power. Baronius thought he'd seen it all before, but the tactics of the Borgias set a new low. Long before the death of Pope Urban, Alfons de

Borgia was offering money, sex, land, and titles for votes. When he was elected and became Pope Callixtus III, it was widely acknowledged that he'd bought the title. Nepotism was another Borgia speciality, and Callixtus soon made his nephew Rodrigo a Cardinal. There would be more family appointments to come. For the first time in many years, Baronius felt exposed and vulnerable. His support for the big-spending Urban meant he had many enemies amongst the Cardinals who would have been happier to see the funds spent on their own comforts rather than art and architecture.

The Age of Beauty moved quickly into the age of corruption and immorality. 'Shameless acts of lechery' were committed in the home of the Pontiff. Once established, the Borgias began to enrich their Spanish family at the expense of important Italian families. Baronius had to suffer the indignity of a visit from the boastful Cesare Borgia who looked around his Palazzo and demanded he hand over two of his Caravaggio paintings, one of them featuring the young Fillide. "My uncle and father will be interested to see this. They both have an eye for artistry of the female form," he sneered.

Scandal was piled on top of scandal when Rodrigo Borgia, father of Cesare, became Pope Alexander VI. A report written during his reign described how 'great throngs of courtesans frequented St Peter's Palace,' with 'pimps, brothels, and whorehouses to be found everywhere.' The only polite description of the Pope's sex life was 'adventurous.' He had many children with his mistress Vannozza dei Cattanei. Another mistress, Giulia Farnese, was known as the most beautiful woman of the day. Baronius lost almost all influence within the Vatican. His work in allying Sicily with Rome and providing money for the Pope was forgotten, but Fillide and Sandro continued to prosper. They were rich and popular because Fillide used some of their wealth to help poor families. A trip to see them was as rewarding as a pilgrimage. The other side of the story was that Sandro and his men kept a watchful eye on the community.

They had spies everywhere, eager to tell tales. Anyone who decided they didn't need to pay for the service was reminded by a visit that always ended in damage either to them personally, or to their property - or both. It wasn't worth getting on the wrong side of Fillide and Sandro. Yet they could make trade better as well as worse, so most went along with them.

"A prudent ruler must not honour his word when it puts him at a disadvantage"
Nicolo Machiavelli

Cesare Borgia had never forgotten Fillide, even though he had many mistresses and affairs with famous beauties. While he was fighting in northern Italy, in command of three hundred cavalry and four thousand Swiss infantry, he found time to send a messenger all the way to Sicily to enquire how her mission was faring. "I have only met her once, but she is the only one I know who can think like a man," he confided to his second in command Antonio Condotti. "She's fascinating: cunning and ruthless. One day we'll find her and put her to work. She can do many things for us."

At the time, he was creating his own kingdom of northern city-states. He was already ruler of Romagne and Marche and went on to capture the cities of Imola and Forli but then discovered a plot against him by two of his leading captains. They were jealous of his success and worried about his increasing power, fearing he would become a threat to their own positions in neighbouring cities. He reacted in a way that set a standard for his future behaviour and his reputation for unscrupulous attacks grew. He sent the captains a letter promising nothing would happen if they signed an agreement and stayed loyal. After a lot of haggling, they did.

It was all a staged deception. Borgia ordered them to besiege the coastal town of Sinigaglia, and when the citizens finally surrendered, he was invited to the victory celebrations. He joined the party, laughing and drinking with the conspirators as his army quietly separated them from their own forces. "I've found a villa by the beach where there's more wine and beautiful women," he suddenly announced. The party moved on, but when they arrived at the villa the mood changed dramatically.

The conspirators were seized, fastened in chains, and locked in the cellar. Cesare left them overnight to ponder what might happen next. In the morning, they were taken to the beach and placed back-to-back. A specially strengthened silk cord was wrapped around both their necks with an iron bar threaded through. The ligature was twisted and turned as it cut into their flesh and strangled them. "There you are," Borgia shouted above their screams, "together to the end! That's what happens to traitors!"

Nobody was safe if they threatened his interests. He arranged to be far away when his brother Marco was found dead in the river Tiber with seven stab wounds. Marco had been their father's favourite son, and he was a danger to Cesare's prospects. Even though many in the Vatican knew Cesare had arranged the killing, he was given command of the Papal Army - a position that had been reserved for Marco. Life as a member of the Borgia family could be short and brutal.

Machiavelli, whose book 'The Prince' would be studied by rulers through the ages, was working with Cesare as a government servant at this time and much of the advice he gave to rulers was based on Cesare's methods. One of his rules was that if a leader has to choose between being loved and feared, he should choose fear. Cesare always made sure the stories of his cruelty were known on the street of Rome.

Following his conquest of the northern states, he made an arrogant, triumphant return to Rome in a grand parade displaying trophies he'd stolen and prisoners he'd taken. "Make sure Caterina Sforza is with us as we enter the city," he told Condotti. "I have a special position for her." Caterina was a formidable and talented woman who had commanded the defence of the city of Forli against Cesare. She performed so fiercely that she was nicknamed "La Tigre" by the citizens. Cesare tried to tempt her to surrender with offers of free conduct out of the city for her and her children. He also promised that there would be no looting, and she could take her treasures with her. Cesare rode up to the city gates to negotiate with her personally but, shouting down from the battlements, she laughed at his offer. "Cesare Borgia, you are one of the great liars of Christendom. The biggest fool in all of the Empire would not believe you. Take your evil poxmarked face away from my gates."

The reference to his face enraged Cesare. In his youth, he had been so handsome that artists had used him as a model for Christ. He offered a reward of eight thousand ducats to anyone who would kill her, but no one tried. Finally, he ordered a continuous artillery bombardment of the city walls and eventually succeeded in breaking through. His troops poured in, stealing everything that took their fancy, and Caterina was imprisoned until he decided what to do with her. At the gates of Rome she was brought to him and he had her stripped naked.

"You ordered me to leave your city gates, and now I bring you to mine. You will have the grand entrance you deserve." She was fitted with a donkey harness, tied to a heavy cart and made to drag it along in the parade. It was a humiliating gesture designed as a warning to any ruler who defied him.

For a while, Cesare Borgia was hailed as Rome's next great leader. He was Commander of the Vatican forces and a proven military strategist with ambitions to unite the Italian states and rebuild the Roman Empire in his own image.

Unsurprisingly he revelled in the scandals that circled around his father, Pope Alexander VI. This Pope had no time for vows of celibacy; he fathered at least twelve children and always had several mistresses. "What a pair we are," Alexander said to his son. "This is the time to be alive. We can have anything we set our hearts on. We are the Borgias."

His confidence had some foundation. He'd served under four Popes. He had talent, experience, and the money to buy influence. On the streets of Rome, he was able to charm the crowds with his oratory. After he was elected Pope, he made reforms that helped the poor while at the same time selling positions in the Church to rich noblemen. His extended Borgia family prospered. Twelve of them were made Cardinals. The Pope's family was growing ever richer and more powerful, but the Church was rotting from within. Alexander's wild lifestyle fuelled the rise of the Protestant revolution. Leaders of the new faith pointed to the indulgence and hypocrisy of a man who was supposed to be a celibate Pope. There were even rumours he was present at Cesare's Night of the Chestnuts.

Tragedy struck, and Cesare's prospects took a dive when his father died of malaria. He was infected too and became so ill he couldn't leave his palazzo. There was no chance to use his charisma and influence the choice of a new Pope. When all the horse-trading was over, the man who emerged, Julius II, came from a family that was no friend of the Borgias - and Cesare in particular. He was immediately arrested and imprisoned.

In Machiavelli's view, Julius would have been wiser to kill him brutally, as an example. 'If you can't be loved, it's better to be feared' was one of his primary rules.

Cesare was dangerous, and he had powerful friends. Predictably, he managed to escape and vowed to return at the head of an army. Cesare saw himself as the one military leader who could bring Italian states together, but right now he needed allies outside of Rome. He turned to a family as rich and powerful as the Borgias had been: The Medicis of Florence.

Their wealth grew out of the wool trade of Florence, and the dynasty prospered with the foundation of the Medici Bank. Where the Vatican was often in conflict with other Italian states, the Medicis were more of a balancing force. But the usually well managed, far-seeing bank made a huge mistake when they refused to give Pope Julius a loan. He borrowed the money from a rich friend instead and used it to buy land wanted by the Medicis. Relations between Rome and Florence broke down, and Cesare saw his chance.

In previous years, Giovanni di Lorenzo de' Medici lived in Rome and was a friend of Cesare's father. In his childhood, he was seen as a possible future Pope, but upon the death of his father

Lorenzo, he'd returned to Florence to control the family's interests. It was natural for Cesare to visit him and propose an ambitious alliance. "Rome will never unite the country, and Florence alone cannot," Cesare began. "Too many noblemen in Rome have different, powerful interests. They bring all of Europe, Spain, France, even England into Italy, and we risk being overtaken. Rome always puts Rome first, but many don't trust Florence either. This Pope will send an army against you and use the Vatican to harm the Medici family. But together we can change everything. For the first time, a united Italy will be ruled entirely from Italy, and for Italy."

Giovanni Medici was tempted to smile at the suggestion. He knew how hard that would be. Yet he gave no sign; he didn't want to make an enemy of Cesare. And besides, what he said was true, so he spoke softly. "Cesare, I have known you since you were a boy, listening to your father as he spoke about important things. I can easily imagine your father saying what you have just said. One day, Italy will be united, but now?" He threw his hands up. Cesare wasn't dismayed by the response. He was a dreamer but not a fantasist. Although he'd been told many times he was 'wild,' his self-confidence didn't waver, so he simply replied, "Giovanni, nobody is expecting this. That's why it's exactly the right time. I can raise an army of one thousand men, you can raise double that. Not enough, nowhere near enough. But it's a start. Let's sit down together, bring your advisers if you like, and I'll tell you my plan."

Over the next two days, Cesare argued, debated, threatened to leave and go it alone. He used all his renowned charm to make his case. Giovanni went for a private meeting with the head of the Medici bank, then talked to his military advisers while Cesare was present. That meeting went well: the Florentine military knew about Cesare and respected his skills. They'd been told about his victories by soldiers who'd fought against him. Giovanni's bankers weren't as worried about the idea as he'd expected. Medici would be in a strong position if they could open branches all over a united Italy. They were easily the most advanced bank in Europe. "We'd profit handsomely if the campaign succeeded," said Tomas Moretti Amministratore Delegato of the Bank. "There's a risk, but Medici could be the biggest bank in Europe."

Moretti was relieved he didn't have to make the decision, but he was an ambitious man and knew a unified Italy would give the bank financial power across many countries. He wondered if Cesare had thought about the economic advantages of his plan and decided he probably hadn't. Which was why he contrived a 'casual' meeting with him in the palazzo where the talks were held. "You're a supreme military strategist with many victories," he flattered. "And maybe, sometimes, you've won more than you know. A victory on the battlefield gives you more opportunities - if you have the right bank behind you. Medici can make every victory worth a lot more; we'll be there to give you financial support. Especially when we open more branches."

Moretti was right: banking was in its early development stages. Cesare knew he needed to fund an army but hadn't thought about the extra opportunities a proper bank could bring. "Have you talked like this to Giovanni?" he demanded. Moretti answered carefully. "Yes, but it will be stronger coming from you." "So you're with me?" Cesare asked. "I work for the Medici Bank, but I agree with what you're saying. I don't think Giovanni is convinced though," he replied, reluctant to spell out a disagreement with the head of the Medici family. "Not yet."

Cesare nodded, happy he'd found an important ally. He brought the idea up in his next meeting with Giovanni. "Think about the branches you can open all over Italy, don't just think about Rome. Other cities have money and when we conquer Medici can be the bank of France, Spain too. Your bank and our army, it's a genius combination!"

His enthusiasm was catching fire as he developed the point and he was moving closer to Giovanni's heart.

"Italy will be Europe's leader again. Think how that will make the Church stronger: united against the Protestants and their sacrilegious ideas." The conversation with Moretti had opened a vision he hadn't thought about seriously for a long time. His motivation was personal power. It was all about him; he didn't want to share with the Church.

But he was reaching Giovanni in a way that hadn't happened before. Watching his face carefully, Cesare saw a light switch on at the mention of the Church's role. It was like a moment of belief painted by Caravaggio. The Medici leader had spent years in Rome, working in the Vatican. He knew the Church faced grave threats from the Protestant movement. The immoral behaviour of Cesare's father had made everything worse. Perhaps he could begin to put that right. Without particularly meaning to, Cesare had planted the idea of the Medicis leading a successful counter-reformation against Martin Luther and the Protestants.

Giovanni bought into the vision there and then. Cesare started work immediately, contacting Antonio Condotti. "We start campaigning again with the Medicis. Find as many of our soldiers as you can, put the word out. Say 'Cesare Borgia needs you.' We're going to unite all of Italy. We've got the Medicis, their army and their bank with us. This will be our greatest campaign ever; we can do what no one has ever done before."

In talks with Medici army leaders, he easily assumed command. His personality and record of military victories carried him forward. Leadership was his natural role, and shrewdly, he proposed they should begin by correcting a Medici setback - in Sicily. "We'll start with Sicily in the south and fight our way north to Milan and Venice," he announced. "Giulio Medici was chased out of Sicily by a gang of murderers and thieves sent from Rome. We'll put that right and send them back to the cesspit in Rome they escaped from."

He didn't mention the personal interest he had in meeting up with Fillide Mellandroni and the plans he had for her: there was no need yet. News of the Medici and Borgia ambitions reached Baronius before anyone else. While he was out of favour with the Borgias, he'd built a network of spies for self-preservation. Like most of the College of Cardinals, he'd been pleased to see a new Pope in the Vatican, especially one as aggressive as Pope Julius II who took the name because of his admiration for the warlike Julius Caesar. But what appealed most to Baronius was his anger and hatred of the Borgia Pope. "Alexander VI desecrated the Holy Church like no one before. He used the power of the Devil to usurp the power of the Papacy. Borgia's reign must be obliterated, his name crossed out of every document." Finally, he decreed, "Their bones will be dug up and sent back to Spain where they came from."

When Baronius heard about the crusade to unite Italy, he went straight to Julius. Predictably for such a short-tempered man, he exploded. "Cesare Borgia, the bastard son, spawn of the Devil, thinks he can rule Italy?" He continued to rage, stamping around his apartment, cursing that he didn't kill Cesare when he had the chance. "I had plans to humiliate him, show the world what he is." As he carried on, Baronius was thinking fast. He'd been told Cesare intended to begin the campaign in Sicily. That was surprising, compared to the northern cities and Venice, the island wasn't important. Then he remembered a strange story he'd heard about an encounter between him and Fillide when she was on her way back to Sicily, and how interested Cesare was in her, swearing he'd see her again when she came back to Rome.

He'd also taken the Caravaggio picture featuring her from Baronius's apartment, saying it was for his father, but it seemed more likely it was for himself. Maybe he could use Cesare's interest in her to trap him and deliver him to the enraged Pope.

"Your Holiness, there may be a way I could reach this Borgia and bring him to you." The Pope turned to him instantly. "How?"

"I believe he is infatuated with a woman who has done good work in Sicily for me. I could use her to entice him."

"Do it!" Julius commanded. "That's the best way to reach a man like him. My Swiss Guard will help you. Do whatever you must. This Borgia does the Devil's work every day of his life."

It was the way back to favour inside the Vatican, but Baronius knew he had to deliver. He couldn't be certain Cesare was really so interested in Fillide; it was just a strong feeling. Yet the younger Borgia had shown himself to be as impetuous and sexually driven as his father, so why not?

Before he left the Vatican, he had a conversation that cheered him tremendously. He was approached by Commander Matteo Brunner of the Pope's Swiss Guard who introduced himself. "It will be my duty to give you any help you need in capturing Cesare Borgia. It is a priority for His Holiness."

Baronius was impressed: the Pope had meant what he said. "Walk to the College of Cardinals with me, and we can begin to plan," he told Brunner. "This is a task I've only just been given." In truth, Baronius had no idea what to do beyond involving Fillide. He called Father Bianchi into his private office, introduced him to Major Brunner, and the three of them sat at his official table, marked with a Cardinal's insignia.

First, he explained Fillide and Sandro's mission in Sicily to the Commander. "I'm sure

Cesare is starting his campaign in Sicily because of her. No other reason makes sense."

"She's a magnet for men," Bianchi explained to Brunner, "but everyone should be warned: men who get involved with her often get killed."

"Well, if that happens to Borgia, we'll have succeeded," Brunner observed. "So how do we get them together?" They continued talking well into the night and agreed that the Commander should meet her as soon as posible.

Cesare's quickly assembled army had landed on Sicily's west coast in the middle of summer. Half of the four hundred men were his own soldiers, loyal to him personally. "Keep them close," he told Condotti. "This new Pope has recruited a special regiment to protect him. I need the same." His first contact on the island was with the survivors of the battle of Ragusa. "Tell me about these men who defeated you, where are they from?"

"Some of them are ex-legionnaires from Rome. They know how to fight," he was told. "They set a trap and surrounded us." Cesare smiled, they sounded like the kind of men he'd seen getting on the boat with Fillide. "How many of them?" "Not many, but they've recruited men from Sicily and trained them. They had muskets and good swords." It was what Cesare expected. "Rome must have given them money," he told Condotti later. "This is the work of Cardinal Baronius. He wants to tie Sicily to Rome. Farms here can supply all of Rome's food, and unless we stop them, they'll take over the whole island."

He didn't know about Fillide's protection scheme, but when he asked about her, he was told she was based near the port of Palermo. Nothing he heard about the 'invaders' from Rome, as some Sicilians called Sandro's force, concerned him. He was confident his men could defeat them. In fact, he was thinking that a series of easy victories in Sicily would be a good boost for morale, and if he allowed them to ransack the villages they passed through, he'd have a contented army at his back. He intended to make his presence felt in Sicily and show that the Medicis were back in strength - and led by Cesare Borgia.

The defeat at Ragusa would be avenged so viciously, no one would forget his name or his army. The small village of Leonforte in central Sicily was the first victim of his campaign. "Let the men take anything they want and provision well for the march to Palermo," he told Condotti. "Make an example of anyone who resists." The small settlement had suffered many raids from Africa and Europe over the centuries, and now they suffered again. Cesare had no plans to win the villagers over. His men were allowed to kill and rape as they chose. Afterwards, he explained his attitude by declaring, "Sicily is a barbarous land. That's the only way to treat these people. When we return, we'll teach them Roman civilisation, but first, they must learn to obey." It was a grave but revealing mistake by a leader who was supposedly on a campaign to unite Italy.

The news spread quickly and turned the countryside against him. Communities retreated and hid. They watched, waited, and planned revenge. Sandro heard about this second coming of the Medicis when he was with his men on a trading mission to the interior and cursed when he heard the name 'Cesare Borgia.'

In Malta, the Knights' Grand Master Luca Albina had a very different reaction and told Giulio Medici he should make contact. The Grand Master had welcomed the forlorn leader when he arrived and saw an opportunity.

"There's a story that Cesare's joined with the Medicis and they're going to try to unite Italy," he said. "But first you must warn him about Cardinal Baronius and his schemes in Sicily. With the army Cesare's got, he might clear out that nest of thieves. Tell him the Knights of Malta have an interest in this and we'd be willing to help."

As for Giulio, he was worried how he'd be received by the all-conquering Cesare. A leader driven out of Sicily didn't have much of a story to tell. On the other hand he was a Medici and there was an alliance between the two families. Maybe he could revive his own fortunes and he wouldn't be empty-handed; he could pass on Albina's offer of help.

When Sandro returned to their Palazzo home, Fillide was waiting for him with Matteo Brunner but she didn't get a chance to introduce him. One look at Sandro's angry face was enough. "I know," she said. "Our nightmare arrived with an army. His men are killing, robbing, raping. Baronius sent word warning us but now everyone knows. The bastard's linked up with the Medicis. They want to take over all of Italy." She stopped short of telling him he'd come to Sicily to find her.

Sandro was shouting by now. "Never mind all of Italy, he's coming for us! He's mad. He doesn't know what he's started here. A lot of people are going to die." Turning to Matteo, he asked, "Are you involved in all this? Did Baronius send you?"

"He's here to help us," Fillide jumped in quickly to stop him from answering. She needed to speak to Sandro alone. Ringing a bell to summon her maid, she said, "Matteo, could you excuse us a moment? My maid will get you some refreshment."

After he left, she poured Sandro some wine. "Sit down, Amore Mio. It's even worse than you think. Baronius wants to use me as bait so we can capture him and deliver him to the Pope. Baronius says Julius hates him more than anything on this earth." Sandro was raging now. "And Baronius came up with the idea of you being used like that?

Are you happy about that!?" he demanded. "Because I'm not. I don't see how it works. Borgia isn't some idiot we can fool. We'll struggle to survive against him and his army. Forget trying to trick him."

Fillide wasn't surprised at his reaction and tried to explain. "Baronius is asking us as a favour to him, but it will help us too. If he delivers Borgia to the Pope, he gets to sit at his right hand, and we'll be in favour too. If he doesn't deliver, he's out in the cold again. Cesare's father pushed him out of the Vatican's inner circle. That's bad for him and bad for us."

Sandro threw his hands in the air. "Baronius helped us, I want to help him. But this? We have an organisation; we don't have an army. If we bring the people with us, we could take him. But it will take years and we'll lose a lot of men. Let the Pope send an army and we'll help him." He continued before she could interrupt, determined to spell everything out to her. "There's something else too. You know our reputation. Nothing good comes out of being mixed up with these people. As soon as they see we're involved, all the accusations will be thrown at us again: we killed Caravaggio, we killed my uncle the Capo and his men, we stole from the Knights of Malta. We'll have a trial, then they'll kill us."

"Julius doesn't know about any of that, and it doesn't matter anyway," Fillide answered. "He's the new Pope. Everything changes when we change the Pope. All Julius will know is we did him a service; we did something nobody else could. I'm not saying it's easy, but - listen to this - the Pope *is* sending an army to help us. Matteo is the Commander of his Swiss Guard."

As he took that in, she added, "Borgia's bad, Sandro, you know that, and dangerous. We're doing it for ourselves." She knelt in front of him and clasped his hand. "Listen, Baronius wants this, the Pope wants this. But we need it. He's only been in Sicily a few months and look what he'd done." Sandro shook his head. She was right, but this was the biggest step they'd taken so far. Winning the battle at Ragusa was nothing compared to this. Cesare would have several hundred men, most of them battled hardened. But he knew they didn't have a choice. He was coming for them.

Philip E. Rowson

Soldiers of Fortune, fighting for the Church

The Pope's Swiss Guard was made up from highly trained Swiss soldiers – they were mercenaries for hire. Pope Julius had seen them in action many times during his work as a bishop in Switzerland. He'd been impressed by their skill and discipline and appointed them as soon as he took office. Most of all, they were reliable. The new Pope realised that Rome and the Vatican were vulnerable, liable to be attacked at any time by forces inside and outside Italy.

When asked why he chose them, he explained, "Every Swiss soldier is a Catholic; they support the Church. They're not just fighting for the money, they fight for the Church."

The force was more than a bodyguard, it was a small army and Brunner had around two hundred men under his command. "We'll join with your force, and anyone else we can recruit to the cause," he told Fillide and Sandro. Choosing the Swiss was a shrewd move by the Pope. The soldiers took it as an honour. "We have good soldiers because we recruit carefully. They're strong and skilful, with good morals," Matteo said. "This is our first action in the service of the Pope. It has to go well."

Sandro's feelings of desperation changed as soon as he saw the calibre of Matteo's men. He wanted to get into action straight away. "Why wait? We'll take the fight to them and frighten the life out of them. Borgia will get the shock of his life when he sees what he's up against, the force we've got"

Matteo, the professional soldier, knew they needed to plan first. "I admire your spirit, Sandro, but let's make sure the ground is in our favour before we attack. That doubles the surprise advantage and before then we need to bring our forces together." Giancarlo Aldati was brought into the planning, and the two forces started training. "Our men can learn from these soldiers," he told Sandro. "This is good, we'll have a real army very soon." After three weeks of work, Matteo was satisfied they had a strong, combined force. "It could be better with more time, but your men are prepared and ready," he told Sandro.

They'd agreed that as Commander of the biggest force, Matteo should be in charge overall. "The three of us will take decisions together," he told Sandro and Giancarlo, "but I alone am responsible for my men, and I will have to answer to His Holiness the Pope for the success of our mission."

"Commander, we're with you," Sandro said with some triumph in his voice. By his reckoning, the odds were well in their favour now. Aldati smiled to himself: he was happy to be alongside the Swiss Guard, but there were hard days ahead. Sandro was desperate to get started. "I'm going to get him myself and drag him all the way to Rome," he told Aldati. "I'm with you," was the quick reply, "but let's see what Matteo has in mind."

"We need to make some hit and run attacks," the Commander said. "Get them worried about what's coming round the corner. Maybe two or three hits then we disappear. Do you want to come with us?" He didn't have to ask twice, and two nights later the three of them were with twenty Swiss guards, hiding amidst some rocks on a hillside as they watched Borgia's soldiers split into four groups and make camp. "That's good," Matteo whispered. "We'll wait to see if one gets separated from the rest." They reconnoitred the area and planned an escape route for after the attack. "In the morning, three will move off and leave one behind to cover their rear," Matteo said. "That's what I'd do; it's a good strategy. If they do, we'll be ready." Sure enough, in the morning three moved off leaving one behind. "We'll let them get a couple of miles away then move in," Matteo said. Creeping as close as they could without being seen, they waited for the signal then attacked on two flanks. Bursting from cover, they hit the Borgia troop hard, catching them totally unprepared. Some didn't even have a weapon close by and the swords of the Swiss Guard cut them down. In the hand-to-hand fighting, Sandro and Giancarlo Aldati were separated, but the Legion veteran knew Sandro was too impetuous and went looking for him as the fighting raged all around. It was fortunate he did because Sandro was having to hold off two soldiers as they circled him. Aldati threw his knife, hitting one in the thigh. The other was distracted by the attack, and Sandro stabbed him in the throat.

A long whistle from Matteo gave the signal to withdraw. Their retreat was covered by rifle fire from four Swiss Guards who'd been held back. The attack had been a success and a message to Borgia. Nobody was injured, and they guessed they'd killed about ten of his army. By the time Cesare was alerted, they were miles away. "They came out of nowhere, then disappeared - fought like soldiers, organised," the group leader reported. "About twenty-five of them; they knew the ground." Borgia told Condotti to keep a twenty-four hour guard, "And from now on we send a scouting party ahead. This sounds like the people who won at Ragusa. We must be getting close." Matteo, Sandro, and Aldati were happy enough with their first mission.

"But we have to hit them again, soon," Matteo said. "If we don't they'll think it was a one off and their confidence won't be affected. Remember, they outnumber us."

Luckily Borgia's instruction to send a party ahead misfired badly and it was a direct result of their hit and rob tactics. Sandro was told where twenty armed men were camped, and men from the local village came to tell him they'd join in the attack. They wanted revenge; Borgia's men had stolen from them as they worked in the fields. The opportunity was there if they acted fast.

Matteo ordered ten of his fittest men to run, make a detour and get round the back of the camp then give a whistle blast when they were in position. This time there was no surprise element but it made no difference. Borgia's men put up a fight at first but they were surrounded and overwhelmed by the screaming and shouting of the vengeful villagers.

To save their lives they threw their weapons down. "Who's in charge here?" Matteo demanded. "Speak up, or these men, the ones you've attacked, will kill you all now."

He gestured to the villagers who stood around, jeering, waiting with knives drawn. One man put his hand up and Matteo told him, "Choose someone to go back and tell your commander all his troops have been captured and now they're going to fight alongside us." Turning to the defenceless Borgia soldiers he said, "If you don't, you'll be killed where you stand."

His tone was without emotion. It wasn't angry, more a statement of fact. The man who'd put his hand up nodded and said quietly, "I'll go."

Matteo's expression didn't change. "What's your name?" "Paulo." Still expressionless, Matteo lunged forward and stabbed him once, in his right arm. "Go now and tell Borgia this is what happens to enemies of Pope Julius."

As Paulo staggered back, shocked and bleeding, Matteo said, "Go, and find out how Borgia treats people who are no use to him." Turning to the rest of the men, he said, "This is no leader; he's a coward. He chose what he thought was easiest. Now, every one of you has the chance to stay and fight with us, for Pope Julius. The chance to be a better man than Paulo."

Sandro and Aldati looked at each other. They'd learned a lot more about Matteo. Aldati shook his head and muttered, "We can't trust them."

"Maybe not, but they're not heroes either," Sandro replied. "They'll do as we say. Look at them." He sounded confident, but he wasn't sure. He was surprised though. He didn't expect the leader of the Papal guard to act like that. Later, Fillide would tell him he was being naïve. Paulo eventually got back to the main force and raised the alarm with Cesare, but he didn't report exactly what happened. Pointing to his wound he said they'd been surrounded by about a hundred men, and he was the only one who'd escaped.

"A hundred? I don't believe him," Antonio Condotti told Borgia. "We'd have heard about that number of men. He's saying that to make himself look better." Borgia agreed, but for the first time, he began to feel doubt. What if Baronius had succeeded in getting more support for Fillide, and now they had significant forces? He couldn't afford to let their unification campaign begin with a defeat.

When Giulio Medici arrived back in Sicily he was relieved to find Cesare friendly and welcoming. "I was unprepared when I first arrived in Sicily," he explained as he apologised for his defeat. "I didn't expect such strong resistance. Everything went well, to begin with, then new forces arrived. Later, I found out they were from Rome."

"Preparation is the beginning of success; it's a lesson you've learned," Cesare answered. "Join us, and you'll learn more. We're on our way to victory." He wasn't certain about this young Medici, but he might have his uses. When Giulio passed on the offer of help from the Knights of Malta, Cesare was immediately interested. "Do they have any local knowledge about how we can locate these treacherous scum from Rome?"

Medici remembered a conversation he'd had with Luca Albina. The Grand Master told him a trader from Sicily had been to see him about the newcomers from Rome. "He told me he'd invited them to the island thinking they could help him, but now he was having second thoughts. They were pressuring him for money. His name was Salvatore Randazzo. He's probably well known. If we find him, he'll be in the mood to help us."

Cesare immediately went to see Condotti. "We have to find this man, start talking to the locals and offer a reward." A week later, Borgia was sitting down with Randazzo, flattering him, offering him inducements. "When we find these traitors and hang them from the nearest trees, there will be a big place for you in the ruling councils of Sicily."

He went on to outline his plans for uniting Italy. "Help us now and we'll include you in those plans." Randazzo was flattered and impressed. Cesare turned on his charm, and soon he had all the information he needed. Unfortunately for Cesare, Randazzo knew nothing about the Swiss Guards and told him Fillide and Sandro had no more than about fifty armed men. "With the force you have here, you can kill them all and take over Sicily. I'm certain of it," he promised. When Cesare questioned him about Fillide, he said she was the brains of the organisation. "She has her schemes for winning people over. She gives charity to the poor and interferes in business affairs, saying she's looking after our interests. All she's doing is looking after herself, and people like me have to pay. If anyone steps out of line, her partner Sandro comes calling with his thugs, and the wisest thing to do is pay up, or she has your home destroyed. They burn your crops and rob you. We can't win against them, but you can. They do as they please with traders like me, but ordinary people love them."

"So, could you take me to her?" Cesare asked. "I want to see this clever woman."

"Yes of course," Randazzo boasted. "She doesn't suspect me; she thinks I'll just do what she says." Cesare told him to stay with them. "And you'll have no more problems with her." That night, Cesare shared a bottle of wine with Condotti. He was in the mood to celebrate. "See, I told you she was clever. We'll bring her with us, then leave this Randazzo to fight his own battles. We move on. I've seen enough of Sicily."

When Condotti heard that, it confirmed a thought that he'd had for a while: They didn't need to be fighting here. Borgia wasn't interested in conquering the island, it wasn't important enough. This woman was the real reason they were here. Cesare had brought them because he was obsessed with her. 'He's mad,' he thought. Like all the Borgias - like his father.

He wasn't competely surprised. He'd been around the leading families long enough to see the self-indulgence. The Medicis were the same; everything had to be sacrificed for their personal whims. As a professional soldier, he just had to get on with it. He was under no illusion about how long he'd last if he failed Cesare.

Randazzo's euphoria at discovering himself in a promising situation soon evaporated after his Consigliere Gian Mariano came to see him, bringing news. "Everything's changed. Troops have arrived from Rome to fight with Melandroni and Sandro. They've got over two hundred men, and they're out looking for Borgia. You've joined the wrong side at the wrong time."

"No, you've got it wrong," his boss argued desperately. "He's joined with the Medicis. They're going to take over Italy, and he's offered me a place alongside him."

"First he has to win here, and I don't think he will," Mariano warned. "But say nothing." He went quiet. His role as Consigliere had never been more important and he chose his words carefully.

"This news will disturb Borgia, make him unpredictable. Maybe it is time to join the other side. If you could find out what he plans to do and warn Melandroni we'd be welcomed."

Randazzo was reluctant to see his dream destroyed so quickly. "Cesare's won many battles, why are you sure he's going to lose?" "I'm not," came the reply, "but there are stories of two attacks against him already. Many of his men were killed in the first one, and in the second they gave up and joined up with Sandro. People say these soldiers from Rome are professional, clever. Of course next time it might be different; Borgia could defeat them. But who knows? So maybe it's best to stay in the middle, say nothing and see who wins. But if Melandroni and Sandro find out you've been talking to Borgia, we're dead. Both of us."

Randazzo knew that, but he was even more nervous about what would happen to him if Borgia won and discovered he'd been playing both sides. He'd heard the stories. They continued to talk, swinging one way, then the other. "Borgia wants me to take him to see Melandroni - and I've told him I will," Randazzo said.

"Well, you can't. That meeting won't happen unless he captures her and defeats their army," Mariano replied. "Why would she meet him? If Sandro and the soldiers carry on attacking, then they just disappear Borgia can't win. Melandroni stays in control."

In the end, Randazzo made a decision. "Enough! I'll ask Borgia why he wants to see her and what his plans are. Talk to him, say we can help him." Mariano thought he was fooling himself. As soon as Borgia found out he was no use to them, he'd be dead or out of the picture. On the other hand, maybe he could get a step ahead and go to see Melandroni.

"So, Salvatore Randazzo thinks he can make a deal with Cesare Borgia?" Fillide laughed out loud when she heard the story. "He's an even bigger fool than I thought." 'And you're a treacherous Consigliere,' she thought as she listened to Mariano. Out loud she asked innocently "Do you think I should meet with him? I've met him before. I know how he thinks."

"That depends on what he wants. Perhaps I could find out," he suggested. So, he's treacherous and dangerous she thought and decided to test him.

"You'd go back to Borgia, say you'd spoken to me and I might meet him? Where does that leave Randazzo?"

"Circumstances change. Now it's me doing the negotiating, and he'd have to accept that." She nodded and changed the subject. "Tell me, how is Borgia liking Sicily? Thanks to our men he's had a couple of big defeats lately."

"I didn't see him myself, but I told Randazzo you had around two hundred men fighting with you. He'll have told Borgia, so perhaps he's not so happy. That would be bad news."

"You shouldn't have done that, we wanted it to be a surprise," Fillide told him. "Better for him to find out the hard way." Mariano said he was sorry and carried on negotiating, asking again if she would meet him.

"Maybe, if I could control the circumstances, and I don't think he'd allow that. Sandro would have a knife in him in half a second!" She imagined the scene and smiled. Thinking back to the time they met, she was sure he was only interested in her as a woman, but would he come to Sicily for that alone? She was curious, and besides, a meeting was likely to be the best chance to capture him and drag him to Rome. "Tell him it might be possible, here in Palermo. Say we'd guarantee his safety. Say we're not interested in killing him or his men - although we could."

"Have you any way of guaranteeing his safety? Giving an important hostage, that might work," Mariano suggested.

"Who's going to be the hostage? Are you volunteering?" Fillide laughed. "Or maybe the Mayor of Palermo would!" she said sarcastically, "Nobody would trust their life to Cesare Borgia."

Mariano was as puzzled as Randazzo about why Borgia was so insistent on meeting her. "Perhaps he just wants you to join him in his campaign instead of standing in his way."

"There's no chance of that happening and nobody knows how the mind of a Borgia works," Fillide said contemptuously. "What's more, I don't care. Go and tell him he can bring ten men as a personal bodyguard. I'll have the same and we can meet in Palermo. Tell him take it or leave it, and again, I don't care what he says. We're going to win whatever he does."

Thinking it through later Mariano decided the safest thing would be to let Randazzo take the proposition to Borgia. If it didn't go down well, Randazzo could take the heat. If it did, he'd have a share of the credit.

Randazzo wasn't pleased to hear he'd been to see Fillide but thought the idea might have a chance of succeeding. In any case, taking it to them showed he was useful. He presented it to Cesare and Condotti as his own. "Sounds like a trap," was Condotti's immediate response.

Cesare stared at Randazzo and asked, "How did she seem? Is she serious? Does she really want a meeting?" Randazzo didn't want to admit it was Mariano who'd seen her, so he shrugged. "It was her idea, but she'll have more than ten men close by."

"So will we," Cesare told him. "Condotti will work something out. Tell her we agree. Let's make it soon." After Randazzo left, they looked at each other, both asking the same question. Cesare spoke first. "Is there a way?"

"There's always a way. They'll be hiding people and so will we. That's obvious. Do you want her alive or will a body do?" Condotti was sure he knew the answer but had to ask. When Cesare shook his head and mouthed "Alive!" Condotti moved into planning mode. "We need to find somewhere we can hide men. Place them behind you, behind her, and somewhere else too. Whatever we do, there will be a fight. We can snatch her for sure but I can't guarantee she'll still be alive."

By the time Sandro got back to Palermo, Fillide had given the proposed meeting a lot of thought and was ready to forget the idea. "I just said it to get a reaction, I don't see how it can work," she told him. Sandro didn't think it would happen either but said they should ask Matteo what he thought.

"It tells us something about Borgia," Matteo said immediately. "He's not thinking straight. He's got big ideas, wants to unite all of Italy, yet here he is working out how he can capture one woman. At least the Medicis have a cause. He's just obsessed with himself - and you. If he thinks he can reach you, he might take risks. Maybe we can use that."

Sandro started to interrupt, but Matteo held his hand up; he was working on an idea. "Hear me out. Suppose we get a message to him from you Fillide, saying you'll meet him: that you've got something important to say but it's for his ears only. He has to come alone. If he doesn't, you won't be there and he'll miss the chance he's been waiting for since his father died."

Fillide was staring at him, wondering what was coming next, but he paused. "Come on, come on, what is it?" she burst out, impatiently. Matteo gave her a half-smile. "See, you can't wait. You have to know. And Borgia will be the same. You tell him you've had messages from Baronius and the College of Cardinals. They're passing on what they're hearing: that the biggest families in Rome, together with the Papal states - Bologna, Perugia and Venice - and the Medicis - all want to get rid of the Pope."

"They're all saying Julius is spending everything on architecture. Bernini's work is beautiful, and one day Rome may be a city of wonder again. But it could also be burned to the ground because the cost is bankrupting Rome and making it weak. Enemies in France, Spain and England are waiting, and Rome is drowning in debt."

"Now, here's the best bit," Matteo loved the next part of his argument, it had only just occurred to him. "Tell him the families have found out the Pope's Swiss Guard is in Sicily and Julius is defenceless. If he's attacked now, they can get rid of him and elect a Pope who won't spend so much money. All they need is a military leader with an army; one that's ready to move now. And that's you Cesare. He has to listen to that!"

Matteo waited again as Fillide and Sandro digested his plan, then he carried on, growing more foreceful all the time. "Now here's why Borgia will believe it," he continued, starting to bang his fist on the table to emphasise each point. "For a start, the most important parts are true. The Pope is bankrupting Rome, and a bankrupt city that can't pay its soldiers is finished, everybody knows that. Julius has asked banks to lend him money, but they say he owes too much, they won't give him more - that's true as well. The biggest bank, the Medici, won't lend to him. So, Rome's most powerful families, the Papal States, the Medicis and the Cardinals themselves all want Julius defeated. And they know it can be done."

He looked directly at Fillide. "You can tell him you know the Swiss Guards are in Sicily because they're with you! And you can tell him if he stays in Sicily, he'll be defeated. An army made up of the Swiss Guard, Sandro's men and all the villagers he's been attacking in Sicily will defeat him. His army will be gone, he'll be dead."

Sandro jumped up and clapped his hands in joy. "I can see that. It makes sense. Borgia is off his head like every Borgia before him, but he can see the truth in there, and he's ambitious. He wants to be higher than the Pope. He wants to be king of everything. But in his heart, he knows he'll lose here in Sicily, he can sense that. At best, he'll be here a long time, struggling. This way, he can imagine he'll win Rome, he'll have Fillide, and he can unite Italy. He's mad, but that's the way he is."

Fillide was thinking carefully. Matteo had suddenly come out with all this. How long had he been thinking this way? Was there even more to this? Had his success in Sicily turned his head? She came straight to the point. "Just one thing Matteo," she asked. "Whose side are you on? Do you seize Borgia and take him back to Rome, or do you join up with him and his army and the two of you march into the Vatican as rulers of Rome?"

Matteo was shocked but he suddenly realised why Fillide was so successful in the Rome of her day. She didn't trust what anyone said, especially people she didn't know well, until she could prove it to herself. He answered strongly, hotly. "The duty of myself and the Swiss Guard is to protect His Holiness, not throw him out."

But Fillide wasn't finished. "The Swiss Guard are mercenaries: soldiers for hire. You could promise them gold, houses, women if you won Rome. Would they follow you, or stay loyal to the Pope?"

"Every man is with the Pope, including me," Matteo answered quickly. "Swiss Guards are good Catholics and so am I." But he'd been so angered by a question that doubted his honesty and loyalty he decided to ask one of his own. "That's me. Where do you stand, Fillide?"

There was silence for a moment. Sandro didn't know for sure what she'd say, his instinct was to trust Matteo but there was logic in what she'd said. As usual, Fillide answered in her own way. "The Church has never done anything to help me, but Baronius has done plenty, and I know he'll always be loyal to the Pope. So, I'm loyal to him. And

I'm loyal to Sandro and his men. Given the chance, Borgia will kill us all and not think twice, so I'm with you as well, and I like the thinking you've come up with. It's very clever. Congratulations to you. And now we've got all that clear let's think some more about the plan. It's good, but it only works if we can get him to meet me alone."

"I know, and we can't say if he will," Matteo replied, "but it's worth a try. His ego is big enough for him to think he can carry it all off. He's a gambler. Shall we try?" He put the question to both of them. They looked at each other and nodded. Sandro added another thought. "By the way Fillide, I'm glad you're loyal to me." They all laughed, but Sandro knew he could never take her for granted.

"We'll have to be open to anything they suggest - to begin with anyway," Matteo said a few days later when they heard Randazzo wanted a meeting about Borgia. Fillide welcomed the Sicilian trader like a long-lost friend when he arrived. The last time they met, they'd argued, but she made sure he knew that was forgotten. "This is our very good friend Salvatore," she said, introducing him to Matteo. "He's the reason we're here in Sicily, and we've worked well together. Don't you agree, Sandro?" She nodded towards her partner; it was important to reassure Randazzo. "We wouldn't have got this far without him, would we?" Sandro played his part and agreed vigorously. Randazzo recognised what was happening, but delivering for

Borgia was his only aim, and he was pleasantly surprised when Fillide said she had some news that Borgia would be happy with. "It's something he's been waiting for, but there are parts of the message for his ears only. I've been given information so secret that if any of it leaks out, the success he most wants will never happen. He can bring a small number of bodyguards, and I'll have some too, but we must speak alone. He'll understand why when he hears me, but I say again, nothing happens unless we speak alone."

Matteo had been introduced simply as someone they were working with but felt he had to spell out a few facts. "I've been sent by Rome to keep Fillide and Sandro safe. I work with Cardinal Baronius, and we have a troop of soldiers here in Sicily. Cesare should know that the biggest families in Rome want him to have this meeting with Fillide and he will hear things that help his future plans. Above all, say he will be completely safe. Tell him The Cardinal swears this on the Holy Book but insists that what Fillide will say is for his ears only. Afterwards, Cesare will make his own decisions. Everything is up to him."

Randazzo was desperate to find out more but ran into a solid wall. "Cesare will hear everything from Fillide," he was told. They agreed to find neutral ground for the meeting and Randazzo left, feeling optimistic that Borgia would be satisfied with his news.

"The promise given was a necessity of the past, the word broken is a necessity of the present"
Niccolò Machiavelli

Borgia was happy with Randazzo's report but took care not to show it. "Tell me about this Matteo from Rome. Is he young? Old? Does he look like a soldier? Is he strong?" Randazzo replied that he was around thirty and did indeed look like a professional soldier. "This is what I expected, and Cardinal Baronius is at the heart of it all. They're trying to lure me in," Borgia said. He wanted to know how Fillide looked. "Is she well? Does she look as if she sleeps soundly?" Randazzo answered that she looked as she had always looked. "She's a controlling woman, that's easy to see. Her man Sandro is strong, but he hardly speaks when she's there. He does what she says."

"You have no idea what this 'secret information' is?" Borgia asked. "No. I don't think Matteo or Sandro know either," Randazzo said,

"Though I can't be sure. As I said, she told me it was something you had been waiting for and that you'd be pleased. It seems to me she definitely has something important to pass on. I say that because of the way she spoke, it was believable. I don't think that part is a trick. What happens after, I don't know." Borgia thanked him for the news. "You have done well. You will be rewarded," he promised vaguely, but it was enough for Randazzo. One of Cesare Borgia's most important qualities was the ability to charm and give confidence to people he wanted to influence. Randazzo had no doubt he was going to finish on top, no matter how this campaign ended.

"Maybe these treacherous Cardinals in Rome are having second thoughts about the Pope," Borgia said to Condotti later as he reported developments. "I hear he's spending too much of their money on buildings, and money is all they care about. I'm going to meet her; we'll have to work on the details."

"Baronius obviously thinks highly of her, so he might let her pass on an important message," Condotti said. "It's a strange way to do business, but who knows what Roman Cardinals will do next?"

As a professional soldier, he had lost patience with the interference of civilians and the clergy in military matters. Privately he was worried about his leader. Their campaign in Sicily was halted, they'd made camp, and Borgia hadn't spoken about future plans, not since contact had been made with Melandroni, and he was sure his unpredictable leader was more interested in seizing her than anything else.

"Are we going to try and take her after the meeting?" he asked. "We'll have to prepare for a battle that's certain." They talked around different strategies and agreed he'd go with ten bodyguards and a troop of one hundred men.

"I'll be with the bodyguards so we can react quickly," Condotti said. "Our main force will be no more than a league away."

"We'll take hostages with us," Borgia said. "Let Melandroni see we have them, and if they try anything we'll slaughter them. She's trying to act like a saviour to these people. Let's see how much she really cares."

A meeting was finally arranged in the Sicani mountains, far enough away from Palermo to satisfy Condotti and in a terrain where he could hide his main force. A deserted farmhouse was chosen, and Matteo outlined his strategy to Fillide and Sandro. "We'll hide men in a circle around the building, close enough to see what's happening. They'll have their main force not far away, but if they try to approach we'll know." Borgia's force was spotted as they moved into position, and Matteo was told they had about twenty men roped together and guarded. "He's bringing hostages. We might have to sacrifice them if they make a move for

Fillide," he said, and Sandro agreed. "Typical Borgia. Blood spilled means nothing." He was in her bodyguard together with nine of Matteo's guards. Matteo himself was in the ring surrounding the meeting. From there, he felt he had as much control as he could expect. "Stay calm, we won't be far away," Sandro whispered to her as Borgia approached with his bodyguard. "Fillide, I knew we'd meet again," Borgia greeted her. "I'm looking forward to hearing your precious message. There are good days ahead."

He dismissed his bodyguard with a wave. "Go, we don't need protection." Sandro and his men moved away too, letting Fillide and Borgia enter the farmhouse together. They went through an open door into a simple kitchen with ancient beams supporting the roof. The room was in half-light, lit by a late sun. Chairs were arranged around a square table in the centre of the room, and they sat facing each other. Fillide, Sandro and Matteo had discussed what they wanted to happen when the two were finally alone together, but they knew everything depended on Borgia's reaction. "The best thing is to get him as relaxed as possible from the start. Give him all the good news as soon as you're together," Matteo advised.

"But make sure he knows you have options. Don't let him think he's in control," Sandro countered. Fillide had nodded to both suggestions. She'd play it her own way and she began directly.

"Cardinal Baronius asked me to tell you there's an opportunity for you to take Rome," she began. "He says Pope Julius is leading Rome to ruin, leaving it weak and defenceless." Borgia's expression didn't change, so she continued. "The Papal States - Bologna, Perugia and Venice – agree, and they're ready to talk with you. So are the Medicis of Rome. Baronius speaks for the College of Cardinals and they're with him too," she paused.

"Is there more?" Borgia asked in a level tone, neither believing or not believing.

"Baronius has prepared the ground," she continued. "He persuaded the Pope to send the Swiss Guard here to Sicily. He told him it was necessary to protect the work we were doing. That leaves the Vatican and the Pope unguarded. You can march on Rome without resistance. But there's no time for delay; soon there will be calls for the Swiss Guard to return." She had delivered the message. She could feel a flush of excitement, almost erotic, as she waited for a reaction.

"So, Baronius betrays the Pope to help me," Borgia let a quick smile cross his scarred face. "How can I trust someone who would do that?" Fillide answered quickly, prepared for the question. "Baronius will always work for what he thinks will serve the Church best. That's all he seeks, and he's afraid that where Rome should be leading, it's failing. The Protestants are growing stronger. Soon they will be at the gates of Rome. He believes that with you, Rome can rise again and be the Holy City, the leader of the Church. He admires your skills: the power of your personality, your charisma as a leader. He believes that Rome needs you." The words came quickly but sincerely; she had to convince. "And what about you?" Borgia put the question with a cynical smile. "Where do you stand in this moment? I can believe in a lot of what you say. I believe Baronius and the Cardinals would do this because they can see this is a failing Pope. They'd lose their palaces, their lands, their income. They want me to save them. What do you want Fillide?"

"I want to help Baronius. That would be best for me and the people of Rome." She didn't have to think about that, it was the truth. She wanted to help Baronius just as strongly she wanted to help herself. She'd gotten used to her power and privilege. She didn't want to go back to life as a high class courtesan, fading as the years went by. Borgia threw his hands up in delight. "Fillide, I want Rome, but I want you too." He moved from the chair and stood by her. "I can do great things for Rome; I was born for this. I won't make the same mistakes as my father. I want to do it with you." The honesty of his words reached out to her, and she could feel his masculine presence, stronger than any she'd known, stronger even than Sandro's. Her body felt it. There was a rush of energy - then she remembered: This was Cesare Borgia. Trying to turn him down gently, she said, "You have many women better suited to that life. I'm just a Marzio whore." Borgia reacted, surprised. He wasn't used to rejection, and fire burned into his words, turning them to contempt. "I know that!" he shouted. "But Cesare Borgia doesn't ask twice. The second time is a command, not an invitation." He moved quickly and pulled her arm viciously, but she twisted her body and slipped away.

She was used to men grabbing at her. Borgia wasn't the first, and she reached down, snatching the knife she'd strapped to her leg. His mood changed again and he almost smiled. "Call your bodyguard if you like, none of you are going anywhere." Then, to their total surprise, Andretti dropped from a beam above, landing just behind Borgia. As he turned, Andretti hit him with a right-handed punch that landed on the side of his face and sent him stumbling to the ground. Borgia was quickly back to his feet and faced Andretti with his knife. "Bastardo!" he roared and lunged at him. Seizing her chance, Fillide came in from the side and stabbed at him, but he moved with a fighter's instinct and slipped sideways. Her move took her too close to him, and this time he grabbed her around the neck. Holding her in front of him as a shield, he faced Andretti and roared, "Stop, or I'll cut her throat now!" He pressed his blade against her skin as Andretti froze. Backing away he edged towards the door. Once outside he shouted for his guards. Antonio Condotti was the first to react - but not in the way Borgia was expecting. He held an arm up. "Aspettate" he cautioned his men. "Wait! We'll see how this plays out." Andretti had followed them out but kept his distance. Borgia's dagger was at Fillide's neck, and he allowed the point to prick her skin, drawing a bubble of blood. "Let her go, Borgia," Sandro shouted. "You'll be safe, your men are here." He gestured to Cesare's bodyguard, but strangely they stayed away.

Antonio Condotti had been running through his options ever since he realised Borgia had lost interest in their campaign. Without his leadership, their army was little more than a mob, and they were facing trained soldiers. He'd no appetite for a long campaign against a force who would hit and run and turn the countryside against them. It didn't take a military genius to work out what would happen. He was a professional with no interest in fighting losing battles for a leader who didn't care enough. When he'd chosen a force to bring to the meeting, he made sure they were men loyal to him. That way he could make his own decisions.

"Here now!" Borgia shouted, wildly impatient and maddened by the hesitation. But Condotti knew this was the time. "Let her go, we don't need her," he shouted back. Borgia swore. "Condotti, you'll regret this. To me, now!" He gestured furiously, and while his attention was diverted, Fillide saw her chance. She broke away, and the moment she was clear, Andretti launched himself at Borgia and brought him down. Sandro leapt in too and together they held him down, face in the dirt, as he struggled and shouted.

Condotti and his men didn't move. They watched as Sandro's guards gathered around the raging Borgia and bound his arms. By now, Matteo had seen what happened and joined them with a shout. He hugged Fillide. "We've done it and you're safe!" He laughed in relief, shook hands with Sandro, clapped Andretti on the back and clenched his fists above his head in a victory salute.

Walking across to Condotti, he extended a hand. "Commander, you made the right call. Take charge of your men and take them home. You'll have a safe passage."

Ten days later, Baronius had an audience with the Pope in the Vatican. He delivered the news with emotion that almost overcame him. There was joy that Borgia was no longer a threat and gratitude for everything Fillide and Sandro had accomplished. "Tell me more about this Melandroni," the Pope said softly after he'd heard the story. "A thread of gold seems to run through her difficult life."

Baronius described how they'd worked together and brought better times to Marzio. "She's devised a system which helps traders, and she uses some of the money she makes to help the poor. She's set up the same system in Sicily and it's beginning to work well. Her work isn't selfless and she can be ruthless but she's a tiger if she believes in a cause. This spirit has delivered Borgia to us, and his Devil's work is over."

The Cardinal left out the awkward stories behind the deaths of Caravaggio, the Tomassoni brothers and Paulo Francesco. No point in troubling the Holy Father with too much detail, he reasoned to himself. Pope Julius gave him the position he wanted, recognising that he'd saved Rome from a disastrous civil war and helped to protect the counterreformation. "You've served the Church well, Baronius. From today you sit at my right hand, pre-eminent amongst Cardinals," he told him, then added, "Be sure to keep Melandroni close. The Church needs fallen angels. Many times, they have the strength their innocent brethren lack."

Epilogue

Matteo made the triumphant return to Rome, taking Borgia back in chains, but Fillide and Sandro decided to stay in Sicily for a while. "I've had enough of the Church and its problems," Fillide said as they relaxed in Palermo. "I think there are as many villains inside the Vatican as outside. Baronius owes us. Now we keep everything we make. What do you say, Sandro?"

"I say we've got enough to pay our men and take a few more on. We keep them happy, pay them well, and we'll be safe. That's the first thing. Then we build up – slowly. No need to rush." Sandro was beginning to relax, he'd taken precautions, had men at his back and wanted to guard what they already had.

"Sure, Sandro. Sure." She knew that was what he'd say: he was never one to search for what he saw as responsibilities. As for herself, she was on a different level. She liked the feel of power. Having money was good; they needed plenty and they'd make plenty. But that was only the beginning. Her idea - earning from both sides of a deal in return for protection - was about more than just money. From her position in the centre, she'd have power and control. She'd be making decisions.

Who knew where that would lead? "From now on, Sandro," she said, "the people listen to us. They need us. The Church can have God. We'll be the Godfathers."

About the Author

I am (surprise, surprise) the father of two highly independent women. My background is as a writer in advertising. I worked for a bunch of London agencies including MC Saatchi and their satellites and invented a line that was used by the company. I had a freelance contract for some years writing one-liners for BBC radio, satire and current events.

Along the way, I've worked in pubs, factories, various kitchens and spent two years in Copenhagen. I now write from West Wales and have self-published several non-fiction books about boxing, a sport I'm interested in (though not from inside the ring!). This is my first serious attempt at writing a novel. I am currently working on another about an American President who, twenty years after Trump, is fighting an uphill battle for his re-election - and crying foul after losing. He's possibly a bit smarter than Trump, though I'm not certain about that. I follow US politics in the New York Times and New Yorker, a mine of good stuff.

Acknowledgements

The publishers and author would like to thank Russell Spencer, Matt Vidler, Susan Woodard, Janelle Hope Leonard West, Lianne Bailey-Woodward, Laura Jayne Humphrey and Stuart Nunn for their work, without which this book would not have been possible.

About the Publisher

L.R. Price Publications is dedicated to publishing books by unknown authors. We use a mixture of both traditional and modern publishing options, to bring our authors' words to the wider world. We print, publish, distribute and market books in a variety of formats including paper and hardback, electronic books, digital audiobooks and online.

If you are an author interested in getting your book published, or a book retailer interested in selling our books, please contact us.

www.lrpricepublications.com

L.R. Price Publications Ltd,

27 Old Gloucester Street,

London, WC1N 3AX.

020 3051 9572

publishing@lrprice.com